SHATTERED FATE

KRISTINE ENDSLEY

ALSO BY

Shattered Fate

The Exile's Paradox Series/Book 1.5

Cover Art and Design by Cristiana Léone

Editing by

http://markedandread.com

Published by KE Fantasy

ISBN E-book 9798989768530; Paperback 9798989768547

First edition July 2024

CONTENTS

To my boys

Index of Common Words

Aeminan— Citizens of *Aemina*

Aemirin— Language of the *Aeminan* people

Ai— Expression or exasperation, like "oh"

Amura Ore— Governing council in *Aemina*

Aore— Senior *Amura Ore* assembly member

Elfe— Elf (French)

Enda— (Elf)

Endae— The elven realm

Fée— Fairy (French)

Hallë— Nolan's nickname for Nevie. Only Nolan uses it.

Imolegin— An *enda's* magical signature

Jumont— Horse (French)

Laro— Father

Meril— An endaen magical amulet

Muranilde— A rare soulmate-like bond Nevie and Nolan share

Murë— Mother

Nol— Nevie's nickname for Nolan. Only Nevie uses it.

Orphelinat— Orphanage (French)

Puce— Flea -common French endcarment (French)

Rosava— Earth

Sajé— A comforting word/expression, similar to "shhh"

Savile— Title of an exile (again, not capitalized when using gender version)

Yalurë (*Yalu*)— Paternal grandmother (Grannie/Grandma)

Yamurë— Maternal grandmother

Zayuri— Org. of samurai like warriors, which Nolan's family is a part of

Word Endings:

-ë— female

-o— male

-e— neutral or title

-i— plural

A note about Nevie's interpretation of French:

When Nevie first arrives she has no clue what the French people are saying, so the French translations aren't accurate. It's confusing for Nevie so it's confusing for everyone and sometimes has no translation, because Nevie doesn't know it. That being said, any inaccuracies are all my own. I can't blame Google for everything.

Remember! These are English translations for the convenience of English speakers. Please don't assume the characters are speaking English just because you're reading English.

For a full ever expanding and evolving translation list, visit my website: https://kristineendsley.com/extras/

1

Nol kicked the thick, crumbly bark of the *Yarada* tree twice, then pulled his legs in close to his chest again. "No way in the realms will I ever be a *Zayuri* like my uncle. No matter what she says. I hate her so much sometimes."

The bark snagged at my curls as I scooted closer to tuck my shoulder under his arm. He only ignored me for a few heartbeats before he wrapped his arm around me, untangling my hair from the tree. We adjusted our position in the palm of the ancient tree we sat in. It was our favorite tree in *Rudairn*, just far enough into the forest to pretend we weren't in the city.

"Don't listen to them. She looks up to Tolwe, he's her big brother." His mother, Wennië, always brought up how she wanted Nol's life to go. Nol inherited the *Zayuri* gene from her side of the family, but my *muranildo's* soul was too gentle to become a warrior who defended the royal family and assassinated criminals. No matter how much he reminded her of Tolwe.

"*Jat,*" yeah, "but I'm not like him," he growled. "*Edeyella racar?* Are you defending her?" His eyebrows drew together, concerned that I'd agree with them.

"No," I said, shaking my head. "You look like him, except he's cold and"—I shivered, remembering my first encounter with Tolwe decades and decades ago—"scary. You may look similar, but your heart is different."

Nol sniffled and looked down at his hands. "You look like Zella, and you're following her path," he whined.

I shrugged. "Sure, but she's the only person who understands me, my magic. Besides, who we look like doesn't matter, you know that."

"I understand you." Nol pouted, tightening his hold on me.

"You don't count, you're my *muranildo*." I dug my elbow into his side until he squirmed. I giggled. "She teaches me more about magic than our professors."

"Because our professors are pompous asses who think they know everything. I hate the way they treat you."

"You do realize your father is a professor, right?"

"Except for him," he grumbled. Not all the professors were asses, just the ones we hated.

"Yalu says it'll get better once I learn to control my magic when I use traditional spells." But the professors wouldn't leave me alone, requiring me to learn how to cast spells their way. They were scared and jealous that they couldn't use magic in the way I could. The way generations upon generations of my family used magic.

"I know, I've heard her. We shouldn't have to listen to them. Everything they teach us comes from books. We can learn everything without their help." He could, because of how quickly and easily he learned things, but the rest of us needed their guidance.

The wind picked up, blowing the spice and citrus scents of the ancient forest giants in our faces. The thousands upon thousands of small conifer needles rustled, like waves of the ocean. The natural energies swirled throughout the air, in the tree at our backs. We could learn so much from the world around us if we choose to listen.

"Yalu says our ancestors taught themselves how to use the Mother's gifts before they could write them down."

Nol shrugged. "That makes sense. Your grandmother is wise. She treats everyone with the respect they deserve."

"But she doesn't respect the professors," I countered, whining a little.

"Hallë, they don't deserve respect. They demand it, and she isn't intimidated by them."

I sat up and looked him in the eyes. "You're not either."

One beam of the dappled afternoon sunlight shone through the forest canopy. Nol's hair sparkled like specks of gold and cinnamon, and his skin took on a deeper golden hue. He looked down at me and smiled, his dimple peeking out. He thumped my nose, knowing I was smiling because of his dimple.

"I can't, not when they don't respect us." I knew he had more to say, but he wouldn't for the time being.

We stared at each other a while, listening to the wind and birds.

"Are you going to accept the proposal?" Nol asked.

I clicked my tongue and leaned back against the tree with his arm still around me before I answered. "Of course, but Yalu and I need to go over the details of the contract, so they can't screw me over like they did her. I can't wait until I'm out from under my mom, though. I'll be able to do things. People will hear what I have to say, and my input will matter!"

"I'll go with you when you leave," he said.

For a long moment, I wasn't sure how to respond. I cleared my throat, tucked myself back into his side, and looked at my hands. "I would never ask you to do that," I whispered. "You want to go north and study."

"*Ai*, there are places to study in the capital, and I'm sure you'll need someone beside you when you've had enough of all those old assembly members. Contracts notwithstanding." He chuckled.

"To become a representative is an enormous responsibility and a great honor."

Many in our family got into politics in some form or another. My father was in species relations for the *Terrin*, and my grandmother was a local government representative. Our government tried to control our family, made us bend to their way of magic, and the only way to take back some of that control was through being a part of the government—we were experts at playing the game. But I had a plan. I was going to change the *Amura Ore*. Change the system and give the royal family more control over the council. Many *endai* supported me, those that were as fed up with their lies and control. It would take time. Centuries even. I would have to pledge most of my life to the *Amura Ore*.

"Did you know they might require me to accept a betrothal like my grandparents did?"

Nol's arm stiffened around me. "They're already talking about that with you? You're not even one hundred and thirty. Who would they want you to marry?"

"Oh, I don't know. It's something Yalu told me—again, contract. They gave her a choice, you know? Between grandfather and another, but if she'd chosen the other, she would have lost her position."

"I didn't know. When did she tell you this?"

"A while ago." I shrugged, but then shot up, catching Nol off guard. "Don't let them control you, Nol. You heard what happened with Yalu and my grandfather, and that was because someone else decided their fate for them."

"Hallë—"

I shook my head and kept going. "You have a gentle soul, and becoming a *Zayuri* would destroy that in you. Never let them make you into something you're not."

Nol placed his hand over my mouth but didn't push. "I won't. You heard what I told them."

I pulled his hand away and squeezed his fingers. "You will never carry a blade."

Again, he stared at me a moment. "You understand me so well. Why can't my mother see who I am as you do?"

I shook my head and reached over to press that worry line from between his brows. "I don't know, but I'll stay beside you to remind you of who you are."

"You keep me true to myself. Thank you."

"Always, you're my *muranildo*."

"*Oyi*!" Gileal, our best friend, co-conspirator, planner, and lookout, called from the base of the wide tree.

Nol groaned and pulled his arm away from me.

"What's wrong? It's just Gil."

"He's been obscenely annoying ever since he scored higher on the last philosophy exam."

I giggled. "You hate philosophy. I doubt you put much effort into it."

Nol shrugged. "I didn't, but—"

"*Oyi*!" Gil yelled again. "Nevie, my love, my heart?"

It was my turn to groan. Yes, he was also my boyfriend, but he always, always laid the romanticism on thick. He let his feelings for me be known to everyone, all the time, even before we dated. He knew I hated it.

Nol laughed.

"Save me." I pleaded with my eyes.

Nol leaned out of the tree and hollered down. "Keep up your copious romanticism and she will run away." Nol looked at me, grinning. "You know you love it."

My jaw dropped. "I do not!"

"Do so. I can tell by the tiny curve in the corner of your mouth. You try to cover it up when you roll your eyes." He touched the edge of my lips.

"No—" I smacked his hand away.

"My endearing compliments and truth will never make her leave me," Gil called up.

I did roll my eyes at that one. Without a smile. "I'm not the one who picked Southern's architectural—oh no."

"What? He didn't—" Nol turned and leaned over the ledge again. "*Oyi*, why didn't you tell me you applied to Southern Ridge?"

Oops.

"I, uh..." Gil paused for a moment. "I needed to find the right time to tell you."

I touched Nol's arm. "He didn't want to upset you."

"He wouldn't upset me with that."

"He would so. You hate the prospect of us growing up and splitting apart."

"I—"

"*Ai*, if you won't come down, I'll come up!" Gil teased.

"We're coming down," I yelled. "You know there's not enough room up here." We would all fit, but this was our space, Nol's and mine. And Gil understood that.

I moved around Nol and leaned out of the tree. The two would freak, but I'd practiced. I knew I could do this.

Go, Nevie! And with that self-cheer, I leapt off, paying close attention to the surrounding air. The wind whipped through my fingers, my shirt billowed in the back like a sail, and my hair swept into my face. I called for my magic to condense the air around me until it could hold my weight, and I drifted to the forest floor.

Gil's wide teal eyes—wider than normal—didn't blink as he stared with disbelief and shock.

"Yes! It worked." I looked back up at Nol, who was leaning out of the tree with his face frozen in terror. "Nol, did you see that? Gil? I did it." I hopped over to an ashen-faced Gil, or as pale as his tan colored skin could be.

"Did what, manage to scare me senseless?" Gil shook me lightly. "You could have died."

"Nah, I knew I could do it. I've been practicing."

Behind me, Nol landed on the forest floor from a much lower branch. He'd gotten pretty good at making that landing. Six months ago, he would have stumbled.

"It could have gone wrong, Hallë."

I rolled my eyes but couldn't stop smiling. "You both worry too much. Don't you have any confidence in me? You wound me."

"Nevie, love, please heed our warning. One day your magic will get the better of you."

I scoffed. "My magic is fine."

"All I'm saying is you shouldn't be too reliant on your magic."

I crossed my arms and glared at Gil. "You sound like my mom."

"Hallë, please at least give us some warning of your experiments," Nol pleaded.

"I don't think it was as much of an experiment as it was a reckless stunt," Gil said.

"That wasn't a stunt. I've been practicing for over a month. And name one traditional spell that could do that."

Nol smirked, knowing there wasn't a single one. "How many times did you fall on your ass?" Nol mumbled.

I gasped and pressed a hand to my chest. "Me?" I looked away and mumbled back the same way, "All but the last three times."

"Gileal, you worry too much." Nol waved him off and started walking.

"Oh? You weren't worried out of your mind? I saw your look." After a few steps, Gil turned and chased after him. Hands on my hips, I stood watching my best friends squabble.

"Come on, Hallë!" Nol called after a good hundred feet or so.

I ran to catch them, scooping up Gil's hand as I got between them, his tan one to my pale one. Nol matched my steps, so he stayed beside me. Today, I chose to up my speed. The day was getting on, and if they waited for me and my short legs, Gil and I would never make it across the city and to the small valley just north of town.

"Come on, Gil or we'll be late," I said, as if I hadn't been the one trailing behind.

Gil squeezed my hand to slow me down. "We'll make it."

We reached the main road, and they picked up the pace that I'd wanted.

"Where are you two off to?" Nol hurried a few steps ahead of us to see us both.

Gil pulled me close and kissed the top of my head. "Alone time with the sunset."

"Does Tiaë know?"

"Yes, my mother knows. And don't walk backward, you're going to fall."

Nol frowned.

"What are your plans, Nolan?" Gil asked once Nol stood abreast with us once more. Even Nol couldn't deny how clumsy he was.

"The Fire Bards are playing at the *Sanrai* pub tonight. This way I can avoid Tiaë and not have to tell her that her daughter and her boyfriend are at the sea cliffs instead of the valley where her daughter told her they'd be."

I gasped! "How do you know?"

"Obvious. Sunset at the valley? Please. You two are my best friends. I know you."

"It's not a secret, Nevie." Gil and I loved sitting at the end of the valley, where it dropped off into the ocean.

"You should see if Rajamë wants to go," I suggested.

Nol curled his lips and scoffed. "Raj? She's so quiet. I doubt she could handle so many people."

"If you're there with her, she'll be fine."

"We don't know each other well, Hallë."

I huffed. "You would if you gave her a chance. She's sweet." And she really liked Nol, not that she would admit it to him, of course.

"She doesn't like me," Nol grumbled under his breath.

"You have this uncanny ability to make everyone like you."

"Not her. I come near her when you two are together and she refuses to even look at me. And by the stars, if I try to include her in our conversation, the look on her face! *Why in the realms is this boy wasting my time talking to me?*"

"That is not true, Nol."

"Is so."

"I've seen the look, Nevie," Gil said defending my *muranildo*. "Though, it's more of a *kill me now and save me from this egotistical knit-wit* look."

"She does not!" I stopped and stared at the two laughing *endai*. "She is shy, that is all. You both intimidate her. What happens is you come over together and—she's not—" I couldn't explain without betraying her trust. "Forget it, don't ask her then."

The trees thinned, until the winter afternoon sun shone above us, the blue of the sky growing deeper. We began passing the more domesticated trees between our homes and businesses. Our tree didn't grow too far from the edge—it was only a five-minute walk to the Tree of Connection, enough to be quiet.

"You're not pouting because of Raj, are you, Hallë?"

"No."

Nol sighed. "*Ai*, I'm sorry, but I won't ask her. Perhaps if—"

"If?"

Nol pursed his lips. "It can't happen, so I won't mention it."

"You have to say it now."

"If you could go, it would make more sense, but you can't." He shrugged and wouldn't look at me because he knew it wasn't my fault.

I pursed my lips. "I could if my murë wouldn't freak out when I even mention going south of the harbor." My mother was the strictest mother in the realm!

Nol tipped his chin up high. "Exactly."

"She won't let me do anything." I kicked a rock, and then another.

"She'll let you clean the house." Nol's eyes crinkled as he teased me.

"Twyn—" I growled his full name.

"Play in the yard," Gil interrupted me.

"Let you cross the street." Nol smiled at Gil.

"Stop teasing me! Both of you. I get it. No Raj—ever, because of my murë. Always Murë."

We stopped at the *greslyn* tree at the head of the road—our meeting spot. To the south of this point was Gil's home at the moon temple, to the west was the main city spiral with the Hall of Knowledge and market, and past that, the harbor. Nol would head in that direction, making his way to the south side of the harbor, while Gil and I would spend the sunset together beyond the valley, northwest of the harbor.

"Why don't you meet me so we can walk home?" Nol asked. Feeling guilty for teasing me, perhaps?

"Before the fourth star on Senna Lane," Gil affirmed.

"Meet in the middle," I said the last part. "Like always."

Nol placed his hands on my cheeks and leaned down, forehead to forehead. Giving in to our bond, my irritation with him diminished. We could never stay mad at each other—the bond wouldn't allow it.

"Now give me a hug, Hallë, so I can go."

He wrapped me in his long arms and squeezed as tight as he could. "She'll let you go eventually. At least she lets you go to the valley with Gil now."

I grunted, squeezed him tight once more, and released him.

"It wouldn't hurt to meet me closer to the pub, would it? Before the third star touches the roof?"

"It wouldn't hurt, no. We'll meet you there then," Gil agreed.

We'd meet Nol at the pub? "You'll take me?"

"Like Nolan said, it wouldn't hurt to walk down. It's not like you're going inside. See you soon, Nolan." Gil pulled me toward the valley, as Nol stayed, waving goodbye.

"Let's find a different place to go," I said as soon as Nol was out of earshot. "One Nol doesn't know."

Gil pulled me closer and gave me a sly look. "Where do you have in mind?"

"Hmm, the cove?"

"No, I won't take you there again."

"Come on." I tugged on his arm.

"No, not until you're—"

"Please don't say older. I've heard enough of that today. Come on, Gil. I thought you loved me." Maybe that was low, but it always worked.

"I do, but I'm terrified of your murë."

Except when my mother was involved.

I groaned. "*Ai*, everyone is afraid of her."

"Except *her* murë," Gil said.

"Don't start. She's coming for a visit for the holiday." I scowled at the road ahead.

"Oh, no."

"Maybe I can stay with you when she comes?"

"I'll tell my parents the situation." Gil nodded and pulled me in to kiss the top of my head. "I'm sure my laro will let you stay in a room."

"So how about it? The cove?"

He laughed. "You are relentless." He held his breath and frowned. "Don't give me such a pitiful look." He kissed my lips.

"Please?"

Gil groaned. "The beach near the lighthouse?"

I looked up and tapped my chin, pretending to weigh the suggestion. "Hmm. Good compromise."

He scoffed and pulled me along. The lighthouse was almost as good as the cove. Although, I liked the lighthouse at night better, and we couldn't stay long enough.

2

GIL BROKE OFF OUR kiss when we heard a familiar and unwelcome voice from the pub's direction.

"Oh, by the stars! Get a room, no one wants to see that," Jemi called out as he and his best friend, Enyco, left the *Sanrai* pub. I knew Nol would ask them instead.

"They may think you're getting a little too intimate with a youngster, Gileal—oh wait, you are!"

Finding that the funniest joke in history, Enyco slapped Jemi on the back and almost fell in the process. In turn, Jemi laughed at his friend's drunken stumbling.

"What are you doing out so late, freckles?" Enyco said after he righted himself. "Does your murë know where you are?"

"That's enough," Gil said, standing up for me.

Enyco snorted.

"There's no need to get defensive," Jemi said. "We're only stating facts."

"That's right. We're just concerned." Enyco pressed his hand to his chest, but his drunken state ruined his mock concern. "We don't want Tiaë worrying about little freckles over here. You know how she gets." They laughed again. Drunk or not, they'd still call me freckles and freak. Only, they'd whisper it if adults were around.

Jemi grabbed Enyco's shoulder. "I can see why. Freckles gets lost in all the crowds, so far below everyone."

My nails dug into my palms as I tried to stay quiet.

"Well, her black hair does help point her out," Jemi said.

"No, they must mistake her for a shadow all the time—like her *yalu*. Two little shadows."

Gil took a few steps forward. The two *endai* took two steps back.

"No, don't, Gil." I spoke loud enough for them to hear me. "They're not worth it."

"What did you say, freak?" Enyco walked forward until he was almost at Gil's chest. "Jemi, did I just hear the freak insult us?"

"I'm not a freak." My nails dug deeper. "You're…You're just jealous you aren't as strong as me." They knew my magic was powerful, and I didn't have to stick to traditional classroom spells out here.

"Please, that's ridiculous," Jemi said, speech slurred.

"Is there a problem here? Jemi, Enyco? Same old insults, same old routine. Want to say all that again?" called our friend Lahiem, walking our way from the entrance of the *Sanrai* pub.

Jemi and Enyco shut up.

"I didn't think so." Lahiem stood right behind them now. "Leave. Both of you." The two scattered away from the older *endaë*. "*Gil, racar astur?*" *Gil, are you okay?*

Gil nodded.

"Don't let them bother you. You're right, Nevie, they are jealous, immature cowards. I don't know what Nolan sees in them."

"They don't do it when he's around," I said through gritted teeth.

"Nolan doesn't spend as much time with them as you think." Carena came up beside her best friend. "They start out together, and then they get bored when they don't understand what Nolan is talking about."

Lahiem grimaced. "I don't think Nolan will be friends with them much longer, especially after tonight. They called you a freak in front of him, Nevie."

"Really?" I asked.

"They asked how he ended up bonded to a freak like you," Lahiem quoted. "Sorry, Nevie."

"It's okay." I tried to give her a confident smile. She hadn't called me that, but I still hated it.

"Nolan came over and sat by us after that. He didn't talk much. But he kept looking at them." Carena pulled me in for a hug. "It'll be all right, kid. You're better than them." She let me go. "So, how was the date?"

I clasped my hands behind my back and bounced on the balls of my feet. "Nice."

"Just nice?" Gil pouted.

"Well, did he at least feed you?" Lahiem asked.

I smiled. "Of course. Where's Nol?"

"He should be along. He got cornered."

"Oh no, go help him!" I waved toward the pub. "He's probably lost and too nice to leave her."

"How do you know he's not enjoying it?" Lahaim crossed her arms in challenge.

"Please. He tries, he really does, but they never can keep up with his conversations."

Carena nodded and Lahiem pursed her lips, knowing I was right but not wanting to admit it. "You go get him, then."

"No, the last time I tried to help, he clung to me and whispered the equation to the *Elendel imolegin* pulse theory in my ear."

"I don't know that one—"

"Do not get me started, Lahiem." I waved my hands at her. "He's explained it to me, and I only understand about half of it."

"At least you know half," Gil mumbled. "He lost me on the sum of *gini* is half the frequency of...something."

I rolled my eyes as I explained. "It calculates individual magical pulses, in order to differentiate whose *imolegin* is whose. Anyway, she got haughty and stomped off, giving me a sour glances the rest of the night. And you know what? He never thanked me for saving him."

They all laughed, but neither of them went back in. I groaned and started to go save my *muranildo* once again, but Gil pulled me back and went instead. They came out several moments later. Nol had his arm over Gil's shoulders as they conversed.

"You two are horrible for leaving me with her," Nol told Lahiem and Carena when he came close enough.

Carena shrugged. "You'll have to learn the art of dating some time."

"I don't need that distraction now."

"Even Nevie has a boyfriend."

"Hallë can't flirt to save her life, it was all Gil's doing." Nol squinted while he teased me.

"Hey! I can too flirt. How do you think I got him to take me to—"

The three others raised their voices to drown out my reply.

Gil's smile grew while they talked over me. "Yes, you did."

"Come on," Nol groaned. "Let's go."

Gil kissed my temple and put his arm around my shoulders. "Are you all right?"

I nodded, but still Jemi's and Enyco's comments lingered.

"Their words hurt, but you know their opinions don't define you."

I nodded again. "Thanks, Gil," I whispered and rested my head against him.

"Hallë, why are you so quiet?"

I lifted my gaze at Nol's question. Nol, Lahiem, and Carena were five or so paces in front of us. "I'm just thinking."

He didn't believe me, but he nodded, accepting my words for now. We'd discuss it later.

"Come up here and walk with us," Lahiem called back.

Gil pulled me up there, but their chatter about the band made things worse. If I was older or my mom wasn't so strict, I could have gone and then Gil could have gone.

"Hallë?"

I lifted my head, only now realizing I'd been staring at everyone's feet while we walked.

"Hmm?"

"Lahiem and Carena are leaving."

The two stood close to each other. The Tree of Connection was just a bit farther ahead. The soft white glow of the magical globes lined the roads. Each root connected us to different parts of *Endae*, and if the rumors were true, different realms.

"Bye." But my mind was on other things, like how accepting the apprenticeship proposal would take me away from bullies like Jemi and Enyco.

"Cheer up, Nevie. If you let them get to you, how will you ever find a way to get back at us?" Lahiem teased as she hinted about how good her prank had been.

"Don't let your guard down, Lahiem." Nol pointed at her then gave her a sly smile. "Hallë and I will find a prank even better than yours." To be honest, Nol and I were having a hard time coming up with one to top theirs. We'd find one though. We always did.

Carena let out a quick, short laugh. "I doubt *that*!"

I tried to give them a genuine smile as they teased each other but couldn't muster more than a quick curve of my lips.

"Hallë, what is wrong?" Nol leaned close, his brow furrowed, as he searched my face as if he could find my problems there.

"We came out and saw Enyco and Jemi picking on them while you were still entertaining the lovely *endaë*. Gil needed help before he did something stupid."

Lahiem nodded, agreeing with her best friend. "They were drunk and tried to get in a fight with Gil."

"I was controlling myself," Gil whined.

"I told them—" Nol swallowed. "What did they say?"

"It doesn't matter, Nol."

Nol was quiet for a while. "I'll talk to them."

"Don't. You'll —"

"Nevie." Lahiem pursed her lips but said nothing more as I glared at her. She was right, telling him never went anywhere. None of them knew what Jemi and Enyco would do to me, though. What they'd done when Nol had talked to them the first time.

"Please tell me what they said," Nol begged. The crease between his eyes formed.

"Don't worry about it. You are all making a much bigger deal out of this than it is. Enyco and Jemi will stop when they don't get a reaction," I told the group, touching Nol's arm as I used our bond to comfort him. Nol closed his eyes, his shoulders relaxed, and his worry subsided.

Jemi and Enyco had promised Nol they'd stop making fun of Raj and me, if Nol helped them with homework. Eventually, they became "friends"—or at least Nol thought so. In reality, if Raj or I said something to Nol—I didn't want to end up in a closet again.

After a moment of silence, Gil squeezed Carena's shoulder. "You two, take care walking home, I heard there's a pack of forest dragons running around here."

Her eyes widened and she looked from Gil to Lahiem to Nol.

"Gil!" I gasped. "Don't scare her. He's lying, Carena. I promise, he's teasing."

Lahiem pulled Carena away from us, promising her that the dragons wouldn't get her.

"You brat." I smacked Gil on the shoulder as he laughed. "They're going to get you back for that, you know."

"That's fine, I have more tricks to use. Speaking of, have you two found a good comeback to their last prank? It's your turn, right, Nevie?"

The pranks started so long ago, I couldn't recall who pranked whom first.

"It is, but there's nothing new to do." I pushed my hair back. My hand brushed my new ear cuff—third decade preparatory honors, three years early. Never as fast as Nol, but I had to work hard to stay in my advanced politics courses.

"We'll find something, Hallë. Weren't you going to look for some ideas tomorrow on your free hour?" He wrinkled his nose. "How did you manage to earn that again?"

I gave Nol the sly smile I always did. "Being better than you at something."

"Politics." Nol curled his lip. "Unless"—Nol squinted—"we skip our class and met Hallë for that hour."

Gil crossed his arms and shook his head no. "You've been skipping too often, Nolan. Your parents are going to find out if you aren't careful."

Nol rolled his eyes. "I get my work done, that's all they care about."

Ignoring Nol, Gil turned and leaned over for a real kiss.

"Enough kissing, you two. And we need to talk tomorrow about not telling me about Southern."

Gil placed his hand on Nol's shoulder. "I'll miss you both, but I truly think this is my calling. We all depart to follow our dreams, but we'll return home again in years to come. It's the natural order."

"I'm as happy for you as Hallë. Don't spare me for reactions you assume I'll give. Please? Contrary to what you believe, I am getting better at accepting change—Hallë." Nol looked at me, using an accusing tone.

I lifted my chin up into the stars to ignore him. The fifth star was almost at the horizon. "*Urro*, Nol, we need to go. I don't want to hear it from Murë."

"*C'yo*! Bye, Gil." Nol waved, spun too fast, and tripped.

I went to catch him, but Gil got there first. "Be careful!"

Nol straightened his shirt as Gil patted him on the back. "Hurry, and no more falling allowed."

"We have"—Nol looked at the wheel of stars in the sky—"several minutes still."

I snatched Nol's hand and tugged to get him running. "We aren't slowing down until we reach your house. Don't think she won't be mad at you, too, if we're late."

Nol puffed out his cheeks as we made it to the *hassop* tree between our houses.

"Do you love him? Like he loves you?" he asked through deep breaths.

"I..." My feet paused along with my words. "I love him."

Nol stopped a step after me. "Do you?"

"It's different for me. I love him, but I'm not ready to make decisions that'll affect my adulthood like that."

Nol laughed. "Yet you were ready to decide to follow your grandparents into politics at seventy-five years old."

"That's different. That decision affects our entire population. I will change things, Nol. Where is this coming from?"

"Changing governments—"

"Nol," I warned him.

"Fine. I watch you two. We've been friends with him for over seventy years, and he has never been interested in anyone else. I don't think either of you know what love is yet. And I am glad to hear you say you're not ready to make decisions like that. I hope that you both consider opening the relationship and exploring love."

"You do realize this advice is coming from a certain *endao* who hasn't experienced any love like that." I leaned over and bumped said *endao*.

"Yes, I know. You all say it enough, but I'm not ready for that. We have hundreds of years ahead of us for finding love. If I have children, it won't be until I'm at least five hundred."

"Like your parents?"

"Yes, they chose an excellent age." He lifted his chin in pride. His parents were almost as old as my grandmother. Nol's uncle was around the same age as her.

"Su—"

"Hallanevaë, Twynolan, where have you two been?" We cringed as my mother used our formal names.

I looked up at the stars. We'd slowed down too much. The fifth star of *Metaela's* wheel was gone.

"I told you, Murë, Gil and I went on a date."

"My expectation is always be home before the fifth star sets."

"You didn't give me a curfew tonight."

"You know the curfew."

"But I was on a date."

"They waited for me, Tiaë," Nol said.

"Where were you?"

"At the *Sanrai* pub."

My mom turned and glared at me, hands on her hips. "You went there?"

"No, I promise. Gil took me to the valley—"

"I don't believe you."

"We met afterward," Nol said. "When the third star was at the roof. I thought that would give us enough time. I was wrong."

"Which roof?"

I squeezed my eyes shut. Nol wouldn't lie.

"The *Sanrai* pub's roof," Nol mumbled.

My mother turned to me. "So you did go."

I stomped my foot. "I didn't go inside."

"We met them up the street."

"Whose we?"

"Lahiem and Carena." Thank the Mother Nol didn't mention Jemi and Enyco.

"Regardless, you know I don't want her over there yet, Nolan."

"I was fine, Gil was with me, Murë."

"No minors should be over there. Does your mother know you went? Don't lie, Twynolan, I will know."

"No, but she's fine with me going there, you know that."

"Do not tell me what I do and don't know. I don't believe you were at the valley, Hallanevaë."

"We were! Why don't you ever believe me? I hate you!"

"I don't believe you because you are always lying."

"I don't always lie. I'm telling you the truth."

"Get in the house. Twynolan, check in with your murë. You know better than to meet so close to *Sanrai's*."

"It was because I knew she'd want to head that way. I compromised."

"The both of you—" Even in the twilight, I saw my mother's face redden. "You know I don't want Nevie down there. You two will be back here after lessons tomorrow. I will find an appropriate punishment."

"He's not your son," I yelled, stomping my foot again.

"He might as well be. I will be telling your parents, Nolan. Now, get home."

"Yes, Tiaë."

"Get inside, young lady, and get ready for bed."

I stormed in the house and headed for my father's study. "Laro?"

"Over here, sweetie. Come sit with me awhile." My father sat at his workbench, bent over a wooden toggle, using his smallest enchanted gouge to carve a delicate design.

"Not long, husband. She's in trouble."

"When is she not?" He raised his head, eyebrows high, as he smirked at my mother.

"You spoil her," she said.

"That I do, that I do."

I sat in a chair and fiddled with another toggle that he'd set aside.

"She went to the south side, farther than she's allowed."

"Ah, yes. That's how it goes. Let me talk to her a moment."

My mother threw up her hands and left the room.

"She never lets me go anywhere," I told him once she left.

He lowered his head back down to his work. "She does it out of love."

"No, she doesn't." Love me, I added silently.

"She loves you and worries about you. Almost losing you—"

"I know, I know." I groaned. "Yamüre reminds me all the time that Murë is barren because of me." My mother hated me as much as her mother hated me.

"Your yamurë is"—my father looked up and lowered his voice—"ancient and spiteful. We must all suffer through her for your murë's sake. You aren't the reason, sweetie."

"I want to stay at Gileal's while she's here."

"Gil's, not Nolan's? What about that girl you've made friends with? Doesn't the moon temple give you the creeps at night?"

I wrinkled my nose. Gil's father was clergy of the moon temple and the family lived there. "That was when I was little. The halls are fun to explore."

"I suppose. You could invite all your friends and explore the grounds. We used to hide from each other at night back there."

"Now that would be creepy. Aren't there old *Terran* graves in the back?"

"Maybe...You'll have to find out for yourself." My father wiggled his eyebrows. "It's an idea, think about it." My dad kissed my cheek. "Now go get ready for bed."

"Night, Laro." I sighed and went to my room without running into my mom.

3

THE COOL NIGHT BREEZE rustled the curtains. Spring would come in a few short weeks, then my birthday three days after. I'd be one hundred and twenty-eight. But now the cold air frosted everything, including my long wet hair. I'd need to close the window soon. Where was Nol?

I threw my warmest blanket over my large bed and let go. My magic caught the corners and I pictured what I wanted, flat and tucked under at the end and one side. I turned down the blankets and slid in. Maybe Wennië would keep him home tonight. Was he in trouble with her, too?

A familiar hiss came from outside.

"Pssst, pssst. Hallë, are you done?"

"Come on in, Nol. I'm decent."

Nol climbed up his ladder under the window. He couldn't scale the side of my house like I could his; he was lanky and clumsy because of his quick growth. Nol towered over all the kids, shorter only than his uncle Tolwe. He climbed over the windowsill in his pajamas, his shoulder blade length hair in a tight braid and ready for bed.

"Close the window. It's freezing."

Nol did so, then climbed into bed with me. Our parents could never keep us apart. Since my birth, our *Muranilde* bond sought out comfort in closeness. Nightmares plagued my sleep since a young age, and only keeping our link open calmed them. Nol and I spent most nights together, alternating houses. We'd spend nights talking, reading, working on homework, or just fall asleep. Our parents got us larger beds decades ago, giving up on separating us.

Nol didn't thrive as a baby, unable to eat much and too weak to crawl. His parents and healers kept him alive, but he continued to decline. Nine years later, the day I was born, Nol ate a whole bowl of porridge. His eyes brightened, and he was interested in the world around him.

Wennië, his mother, brought Nol over several days after my birth, excited for her best friend's successful birth and to show my mother Nol's improvements. Nol managed to find my crib and pulled himself up to me. In the evening, she took Nol home, amidst his pleads to stay. He almost died that night. Wennië ran back to our house, and he started breathing the moment he came close to me.

Nol's cold feet touched mine and I squealed.

"They're not that cold, don't be so dramatic."

"They're numb. You better check them for frostbite."

Nol groaned. Who was the dramatic one now? I giggled, which got Nol going as well. We settled in and stared at my dark ceiling.

"How bad did they tease you?"

I licked my lips. "I don't want to talk about it."

"They told me they didn't mean any harm. I thought...I thought you were overreacting."

"Like you always do."

"I'm sorry. It's just that you do! I wish you'd tell me what they said."

"It doesn't matter."

"It does so."

"Why? What would it change? Would you go defend my honor? Sic your uncle on them?"

"That's not—"

"Just stop. You've been busy, and I didn't want to distract you. Besides, it would make things worse."

"You're my *muranildë*, nothing is more important."

"No, that isn't the point of these lives together."

"Then what do you think is?"

"I don't know, but what would be the point for always—" I growled. "I don't know."

"Why do we die if we're not alive at the same time?"

"You know as much as me."

Which wasn't much.

Nol sighed. "You've always had more incite than I on this bond."

"I just...say what makes sense. If you'd get your head out of books, you'd have time to contemplate the meaning of life as well."

"Maybe if you put your head in books more often, you'd get better marks."

"That's what you're supposed to be for."

He found my feet with his icy ones and held on. I squealed again and he laughed.

"See—we have our purposes. You focus on philosophy and share your results, and I'll help you study."

"When was the last time you helped me study? I told you Raj and I needed help with math, and you never showed."

"She wouldn't stay if I came."

"She will so. She's funny—quiet, but funny. And sweet. I think you'd like spending time with her."

Nol tugged on my hair. "She's slow and way too cautious."

"Maybe we need some caution."

"You? Caution? You'd cease to exist."

"Just give her a chance. We need help with our math test at the end of next week. Do you think you could peel some time away from your busy life for a little study time tomorrow?"

"Tomorrow? No. I already made plans. I don't know about the day after either—and before you ask, we can't the day after that. Remember?"

"Yes, yes." I rolled my eyes, groaning. "We're all going foraging for your mom's dye ingredients."

"Don't act like that. We always have fun."

"I'm just frustrated with you about—"

"Raj," he groaned.

"Oh, is that a chore for you?"

"I didn't say that."

"I can read your mind."

"Cannot—"

"Hallanevaë? Twynolan? Are you two still awake?"

I wrinkled my nose and shook my head no.

"We are, Tiaë."

"An'di's here. She says Wennië needs you home."

"Oh...all right. Coming." Nol flipped the covers back and got out of bed.

"I'll head over later."

"No, go to sleep." The light from the window cast his body in darkness as he stood next to the bed still. "We stayed up far too late last night. I almost fell asleep in history."

I scoffed. "You always fall asleep in history."

"You've been sleepy all day, too. Get some rest."

"Yeah, but—" I swallowed hard.

"You'll be fine. Besides, we are getting older. You can fall asleep by yourself."

"That's not it. What if I have another nightmare."

"You haven't had one all week. Let's try it."

"But they might come back."

"Well, if it does, come over."

"But I...I get scared after them. I don't think I'll be up to coming over."

He flipped the covers back and patted my shoulder. "You'll be fine."

"Nol." I couldn't help but whine.

"You are a pain in my ass."

I sat up and smiled. "Not as much as you are in mine."

He tapped my nose as An'di opened the door. She conjured a dim light inside the sconce on my bedroom wall. I squinted as my eyes adjusted. "Hey, brats. Nolan, come on. Murë and Laro want you home. Looks like you've got some explaining to do."

"Great." He looked at me, eyes wide. "It wasn't that big of a deal. What's so wrong with you meeting me there? It's not like you were alone."

I shrugged, not getting my mother's issue with our night out either. And now she'd brought his parents into it.

"What are you talking about?" his sister asked. "Come on, get your shoes on."

"Tiaë and her overbearing tendencies," he explained to her. "Now Murë and Laro are irritated because she made it sound so dire."

"No clue what you're talking about, little brother. But they found out you skipped classes today. They want to know where you were." She crossed her arms.

"Did you tell?"

"No," An'di answered her brother.

"You skipped and didn't tell me?" I whined.

"You said you can't skip any more classes."

Curse the school and all that learning.

"Your marks are horrible," Nol reminded me. "You have to go."

"Only in casting, and I don't care about spells. Professor Asin was a jerk today. How does everyone remember all the hand placements? Ugh, so boring," I said.

An'di put her hands on her hips. "You need to learn them all the same."

"She's horrible at placements. They're just pissed because she doesn't have to use them to get results." Nol turned to me. "Still, you have to get through this or they'll never pass you, and then you'll never get into that apprenticeship."

"I know," I grumbled. "I'm getting better. I have most of the spells on the test memorized."

"Do they work for you though?" An'di asked.

"Sometimes. I'm so frustrated, and my way turns out just as good as theirs. It's just simpler...and faster...and they're jealous."

"Maybe if you'd show some humility"—An'di glared down at me—"they'd be more open to alternative ways. You need to compromise, Nevie. You're faster, yes, and stronger, but that doesn't mean you're better than them."

"I don't think I'm better than them."

"Why'd you embarrass Professor Rassel the other day then?"

"That was something completely unrelated."

"Hmm. We can talk about this later. If I don't see you tomorrow, I'll see you after Zella and I get back from *Casbrin.*"

My grandmother was taking An'di to the university in *Casbrin*, a few days north of here, visiting the campus and staying for a lecture on herbal medicine. How was that any fun?

"Night, Nol." I lay down and covered my head.

He pulled the blanket down and rested his head on the pillow, placing his hand on my cheek. "Try to sleep on your own tonight. Please?"

I nestled into this hand and closed my eyes. "Fine. You're going to sleep like garbage tonight, though."

"Will not." He kissed my forehead. "Night."

"Come on, brat," An'di called from the hall.

Once I couldn't hear them talking from out my window, I stared at the ceiling. Nol was right, I hadn't had a nightmare in a week.

"No nightmares tonight." I squeezed my eyes tight. "Leave me alone," I whispered to my unconscious.

I COULDN'T CATCH MY breath.

Running.

Through the woods, past dark trees reaching for me.

Something chased me. What?

Dare I look back? What if I saw it?

Drawing up my courage, I turned around. An eyeless, noseless tall white being with thin, sticklike limbs ran after me. Its huge mouth, taking up half of its face, was gnashing its sharp, needlelike teeth. Its long legs ate up the distance between us.

I screamed, then stumbled. Sticks punctured my palms as I slammed onto the forest floor. I rose to my knees and looked at my hands. Blood gushed out of holes, widening as I looked down at them.

The being snarled right behind me. I tried to get up, but my long pajamas tripped me.

My chin slammed into a root.

The holes in my hands pushed my fingers apart. My pinkies fell off.

I screamed and cried.

The thing clamped on to my shoulder and bit down on my neck.

I woke up in a cold sweat. My mom had my shoulders, shaking them to wake me and crying. My father sat at the foot of my bed, holding my feet still.

"Murë? Laro?" I swallowed and choked on my spit. "I'm sorry," I cried and coughed. "Why won't they stop?"

"Oh, baby, I don't know." My mom hugged me, pulling me in as tight as she could.

"Don't be sorry, Nevie. This isn't your fault." My dad rubbed my feet and ankles.

"But I hate waking you up," I bawled.

My mom pushed my hair back, lifted it in the back, over and over again. "If I could take them for you, I would. In a heartbeat."

"I want Nol." I sobbed into my mother's shoulder.

"*Sajë, esmë'a. Sajë.*" *Shh, my love. Shh.* "He's asleep at home. Would you like to come sleep with us?"

But that never worked. I shook my head. "You can't calm them like he can. I'd only thrash and hit you if I have another one. I just want them to go away."

"We'll stay here. Maybe we can wake you quicker if we're here."

"I'm so sorry."

They both lay down beside me—my dad behind me, my mom in front, rubbing my back and holding me. My hiccuping subsided, and I fell back asleep between them. There were more nightmares, but not bad enough to wake us.

4

MY WARM BREATH BILLOWED bright white in the cold morning air. I hated getting up so early. The birds sang so loud my ears rang. Why couldn't lessons start at midday?

Nol and I met next to the *hassop* tree. His hair bounced along behind him and his knee-length wool coat caught the air as he almost sprung in the air with every step. He hitched his large leather pack higher up his shoulder, full of books by the look of it.

"Morning." He almost smiled at me. Smiled. Before sunrise. But it didn't reach his eyes, revealing his fake happy morning greeting.

I mumbled a reply, my first time talking this morning.

"Did you have a nightmare?"

"Yes," I snapped.

He frowned, unwilling to believe me. "Did not."

"Did so." I squinted, but I couldn't stay mad at him. "How'd you sleep?"

He wrinkled his nose. "Fine." Liar. Nol rested his arm on my shoulder as we began walking to the Hall of Knowledge.

"Then why are there bags under your eyes?" I squinted at him. "And yes, I did have a nightmare." But as dreams always went, I couldn't describe it.

Nol grumbled. Nightmares plagued my sleep, but Nol never slept well without me, either. I tucked myself closer beside him. We'd get through the morning together.

"Nevie, my love!" Gil stood at the crossroads, with his crooked smile and hands in the pockets of his short leather coat. The wind tangled his untamed, coarse hair as he waited for us. His smile faltered as we came closer and he saw our unhappy faces. "Uh, oh. I thought you were supposed to stay at her house last night, Nolan."

"I did, but Murë and Laro called me home."

"Why didn't you go with him, love?"

"Nol wanted me to stay home."

"Your attempt at distancing?" Gil asked Nol as pushed his hands farther in his pockets. "How'd that work for you? Every time you two sleep separately, this happens, and I don't get snuggle time with my girlfriend because you two need to recharge."

"Sorry, Gileal," Nol said, only half serious.

Gil rolled his eyes and took his spot beside me. "How will you two survive apart? We need to figure something out. You can't spend all your lives sleeping at each other's houses."

"I will always be beside her."

"Not literally, I hope. I love you, Nolan, but not enough to take you with us when Nevie and I take our trips around the world. You also won't sleep in the same bed as us."

"I see you changed our plans for the future?" I teased Gil.

"Yes, as a matter of fact. We will go on our own journeys, the three of us. Come home every summer to be together, then you and I marry when you are five hundred fifty-nine years old."

"Oh? That's an interesting number." I tried not to laugh as the two of them began to change my mood.

Later, once Gil experienced the world more, he'd change, grow, and realize we wouldn't stay together forever. I loved him, but...we had different fates. I needed to stay at the capital. Gil wanted to explore, build and repair buildings, come back and live here in *Rudairn*. And if his father had his way...Gil would take over as the clergy to the moon temple.

Gil laughed. "It just came out. But now I must leave you. Morning lessons await."

I hadn't even realized how far we'd walked. Across the city center's spiral, The Hall of Knowledge loomed, a large building that contained the city library and our school system. Primary learning took place on the left behind the library. The full right side was dedicated to secondary education to prepare us for universities and apprenticeships.

I snatched Gil's hand before he could get too far. "Why don't we skip class and get sweet rolls instead."

"No," Nol scoffed. "I don't want to piss my parents off for a few days, at least. They let me off easy, since Tiaë is punishing us today."

"What did you do?"

"Oh, I got in trouble for going past the harbor, and Nol got in trouble because we met him there," I answered before Nol could. "And she thinks I'm lying that I didn't go into the pub."

"Oh, and she doesn't believe that you two went to the valley," Nol added.

"*C'yo,*" Gil swore. "That makes no sense. What if I vouch for you?"

"Don't put yourself in the middle of this. We must take our punishment for *not* doing anything she didn't want us to, with grace and maturity."

I scoffed. "We don't even know what she wants us to do tonight. I can't stand her!"

"You'll get along later in life." Gil and my mother got along in an odd sort of way.

"Much later," I grumbled. "Maybe."

"I must be off, take care of Nolan my love. I hope you two have recharged enough to keep him from being grumpy in class." Gil moved so he could kiss me.

"Not here," Nol teased. When I got Raj and Nol together, I'd repeat that back whenever I got the chance. Gil let go of me and walked backward until he made it to the steps.

My stomach growled.

"We'll get food after class," Nol promised after Gil ran up the stairs.

"Maybe. If Professor Hanno lets us out on time." She always kept classes to the very last second.

"Or you could leave early and bring some back. Hanno would let you if you brought her one, too. That's what assistants are for, right?"

"Hmm. Depends on her mood."

"Nevie?" Professor Hanno called me over as everyone else hurried out after class.

"I'll run and get breakfast," Nol offered. He stepped away, walking backward, and bumped into a table.

I cringed. "Be careful and don't run too fast."

"I'll be fine." And yet, he bumped into another table.

"You broke your wrist last time." I stood at Hanno's desk, calling out to him as he got to the open doorway.

Nol waved me off and hurried out the door.

"That *muranildo* of yours. What will you do with him?"

"I don't know."

She smiled, but she looked nervous. "I wanted to discuss a good time to bring up your study abroad plans to your parents."

My stomach dropped at the mention of my parents. "I don't think it's going to happen. I can't get ahead in magical studies."

She nodded. "But you're ahead in every other class. They can't hold you back for your magic...differences."

My magical studies professors didn't see it that way. "Thank you. That means a great deal to me."

"I heard back from *Pequwyn*."

My stomach flipped. Quick answers meant no. "Already? They have decades to consider me."

"You need more challenges, and I explained that. You're fluent in *Pequwynian*. You've translated all of my *Mellorian* books into *Aemirin* and *Pequwynian*. Not many *endai* get a chance like this."

I nodded. "So, is that a yes or a no?"

She smiled. "They'll be sending a proposal to you soon."

"They have forever to do this." But I couldn't stop smiling.

Hanno's exhale shook. "The *Pequwynin* professor and I think it would be wise to accept an abroad proposal before your apprenticeship."

"Why before?"

"You didn't hear this from me." She shook her finger at me and waited until I nodded. "The *Amura Ore* is getting nervous that you haven't accepted yet."

"I have until I'm one thirty to decide." My bag slipped off my shoulder and my stomach growled again.

"They're worried about your progress in magical studies."

I crossed my arms at her hedging.

"They want you as soon as you accept."

"What?" I wanted to get away from here, but leaving my friends now? I ground my teeth. "And if I say no?"

Hanno licked her lips. "You need to be careful, Nevie. The *Amura Ore* isn't to be trifled with."

"So choose the abroad proposal...then the capital's...to prevent the *Amura Ore* from taking me before I'm one fifty?"

"I can only hold them off for ten years."

"Leave before I'm one hundred and forty years old?" My voice echoed through her room.

"*At* one forty—let's get together with your parents and get it sorted out."

"I need to process this, and I want to talk to Yalu before my parents." Or rather, my mom. My dad understood politics—growing up with assembly members for parents did that. "She could find out more..."

"That's a smart idea. Zella will know how to ask discretely."

"Hallë?" Nol called from the door, breathless and holding up a paper package. "We need to go!"

"Oh dear, I'm so sorry, Nevie. Let me write you both a pass, and you can take your time eating your breakfast."

I followed Hanno over to her desk to receive our passes while Nol ripped the package open at the door and started eating without me. The brat. I gave the professor a quick wave and dashed out the door.

Nol and I walked down the stairs together, ripping pieces off our rolls.

"Hallë?" Nol tugged on my hair. "Hallë?"

"Ouch, what...Nol? Stop."

"I called your name five times. Where did you go? What'd she want?"

I shoved another bite into my mouth. "Well, I need to process—"

"*Alluot*, I'm your *muranildo,* you tell me everything."

"Don't cuss like that. See what I mean about Jemi and Enyco?"

He tilted his head as I nagged. "You're not going to distract me, Hallë. What did she say?"

"You aren't going to like it. There's change involved."

"*Tulla—*"

"Twynolan, you stop cussing! Anyone can hear you."

He lifted an eyebrow, waiting. I huffed. "Fine! It's about studying in *Pequwyn*. If I do it, I'd need...to go before I move to the capital."

Nol shoved a piece in his mouth. "How soon?"

"It's a five-year program. So..."

"Oh." He puffed out his cheeks and tilted his head back. "How long have you been talking about going to *Pequwyn*?"

"She brought it up...in the fall."

His brow furrowed. "But yesterday, when I said I'd go with you...why didn't you say something?"

"I wasn't thinking of it. You've talked about different universities, so I was focused on your choices. I figured none of you would be with me in the capital, so it's just as well to visit *Pequwyn*."

"Right." He knew I wasn't saying everything.

"I haven't said yes—to any of it."

"But you will."

"That's not—I don't know. I told her I wanted Yalu to see what the *Amura Ore's* stand on it is."

"What do you mean?"

I explained what Hanno said. "Are you mad?"

He shook his head, his cinnamon-red hair brushing the sides of his face. "I'll need to...process this."

"See? That's what I said."

Nol smiled as he headed off down the hall, away from me toward his classroom. Exasperated, I kept walking and ate my roll, unconcerned about how much of the lesson I missed.

Raj's deep periwinkle eyes went wide as I stepped into my mathematics lesson, producing my note out of my pocket as our professor scolded me. I didn't pay his words any bit of attention, but Raj's face darkened as I walked to my desk beside her.

"Hallanevaë!" Professor Rassel yelled after me.

Startled, I jumped and smacked my hip into the corner of a desk. "What?"

"Do not talk to me in that tone of voice, young lady."

"Then don't yell at me like that. I've done nothing wrong."

"You are late. Again."

"Yes, and this time I gave you a note."

"And I'm supposed to believe this is real?"

"Why wouldn't it be? I didn't give you one yesterday when I came in late after a mishap in the bathroom."

The other students gave a nervous chuckle. Sure, a bit embarrassing for me, but it happens to every female of every species.

"Which was also unacceptable."

"Fine. It's unacceptable, but still unavoidable. And if you don't believe me about today, you can go ask Hanno. It's not my problem if you believe me or not." I set my bag next to Raj and smiled at her.

"Leave."

"Excuse me?" I froze.

"Leave my room."

"Why? Because I was late? With a note from Hanno?"

"I will confirm your note later and excuse your absence for today if it is legitimate."

"My absence? I'm here, ready and willing to learn."

"You are just as obstinate as Nolan."

"So?"

"Leave my classroom, Hallanevaë."

"And go where? I'm supposed to be here."

"You should have thought about that before you so disrespectfully interrupted my lecture."

"It wasn't my fault."

"To the headmaster, now."

"This isn't fair."

"And you continue to disrespect me and disrupt your classmates' education. The students who came in on time."

"I'm not the one making a big deal out of it. You're the one who chose to yell at me, instead of ignoring me so I could walk in quietly."

"Hallanevaë, if you don't leave right now, I will suspend you for two weeks."

Twenty days in a row? I wouldn't be able to catch up. Everyone stared from me to the professor and back. I yanked my bag off my desk and got my butt out of class, but I turned under the entrance. "I want my note so I know you won't rip it up and try claiming I didn't have one."

"I wouldn't do that."

"Right. Like you did the last time I gave you one? I got a full week of detention because you threw it away."

"How dare you, you obstinate, disrespectful, self-centered little—child!"

I glared at him, knowing what he wanted to say. Freak.

"If you try to claim I didn't give you a note, Hanno will vouch for me and everyone here is a witness."

I was out the door before he uttered suspension again. I left like he told me to, when he told me to. I hated math. I hated these teachers. Maybe I would go to *Pequwyn*—the sooner, the better.

5

"NEVIE!" RAJ WHISPERED, FINDING me in the library during my free hour. "*Urro*, I can't believe you stood up to him. Professor Rassel was so mad. He did throw away your note, right after you left."

"*Sitaconem ni*!" *I knew it*! I squeezed my hand into a fist.

A rustling of paper brought my eyes back to her. "But I took it out when I left. Ayla and Fellë helped distract him."

"*Ai*, you—they all did that for me?"

She nodded, smiling like a loon. "Everyone is talking about it. Did you go to the headmaster's office?"

"Yeah."

"What did he say?"

"Nothing. I'm supposed to stay after lessons to talk and have a big meeting with Rassel and my parents. My murë wanted me home right after lessons."

"Did you tell him that?"

"Yes. Then he said I shouldn't have acted out in class. But Rassel yelled my name across the room, and I refuse to back down from that kind of treatment."

"You told him all this?"

"Yes."

"And?" Her eyes widen and she almost vibrated with energy as she waited for my answer.

"I still have to meet them at the end of the day."

Raj deflated and her mouth dropped. "What about Professor Hanno?" .

"What about her?"

"Can't you ask her to defend you?"

"This isn't her problem. She kept me late, but he didn't have to react like he did." I pulled Raj in for a hug. "*Perudar lyenoso nafela ryaen seta.*" *Thank you so much for returning this.* "I can't wait to pull this out once he claims I didn't have one."

"You're welcome. I wanted to ask. Did you go to the cove last night? I'm not certain if I dreamt it or had a vision."

"We went to the lighthouse beach."

"Oh, so dream."

"Well, the cove is on the beach. You say visions are always changing, and the ones of mine are always tangled and twisted up."

"True. There weren't any pirates in pink?" She giggled.

"Definitely a dream. I tried to convince Nol to study with us tonight or tomorrow, but he had made other plans."

Raj deflated. "It's fine. He doesn't like me. I understand."

"He doesn't know you, yet."

"No one wants to be close to me. I make them uncomfortable."

"Not me!" I got a *shh* from the librarian.

"No, because your fate is so crazy, I can never tell what is most likely to happen."

"Pink pirates?"

"Exactly."

I looked at her deadpan.

"Well, okay, they weren't pink—but the sunset had pink in it. The pirates were there in some capacity. They could represent something else. Night visions are weird. I'm confused on how it all fits together."

"Don't push it. I'm confusing, we've established this."

"Yes. So to lessons I go. Good luck with the meeting."

"So you kicked my daughter out of the room after she gave you that note from another professor?" my mom said.

Professor Rassel stuttered, looking down at the note the headmaster now held.

"She never gave that to me."

"Liar." I bolted out of my seat. "The entire class saw me give it to you. Raj pulled it out of your trash basket. They all watched you throw it away after you kicked me out."

"Hallanevaë, calm down," my dad said, tugging on my shirt to get me back in my seat.

"Rassel?" the headmaster asked.

"She's a troublemaker and has no respect."

"That doesn't excuse your fault in this. You lied to our faces. You told me Nevie didn't bring you a note, yet several of your students informed me that she gave you a note."

"What?" Rassel's eyes bulged out. "You talked to my students?"

"Or course I did. I'm tired of hearing about Nevie's constant misconducts. Yes, she's trouble, but you complain about her constantly. She can't possibly be that bad. You and Professor Asin always tell me how much trouble she and Nolan are. What do you want me to do? Kick them out so you don't have to deal with them?"

"N-no."

"Nevie, you, my dear, need to stop giving Professor Rassel and Professor Asin such grief. Professor Rassel, I expect you not to mark her absent for today. Nevie, you will have noon detention tomorrow, and the first two days after you get back from the weekend break, for speaking to Professor Rassel so disrespectfully."

"But he shouted—"

"Nevie," my dad warned.

"If you don't want your professors shouting at you, acknowledge them when they speak to you—respectfully."

I scowled and slouched back in the seat. Like Nolan said, why should we give them respect if they didn't give us any?

My mother steamed all the way home. About the professors, me, Nol. Life with me in general. My dad kept me close, tucking me under his arm and then squeezing my shoulder. We turned the corner to our street and passed Nol's house. Ours came into view after we passed the wide *hassop* tree. Wennië made us harvest the nuts for her brown-black fabric dyes. *Hassop* trees didn't grow as tall as the ancient *coyana* trees—which grew so high the clouds hid the canopy—but their thick branches were twisted, creating ledges to stand on after climbing their knotty bark.

Nol sat on the second step in front of our house. When he saw the three of us, he sprang up to run, but tripped over his feet and fell on his side. I hissed in sympathy. Everyone said his muscles would catch up and he'd balance out. He'd outgrow his uncle soon if he kept it up. It had to stop somewhere.

Mom reached him a step before we did. "Twynolan, you must be more careful, sweetheart."

"Yes, Tiaë."

"Now, the both of you, get in here."

"But, Murë—"

"You thought you were going to get out of punishment because of that? I don't think so."

"Laro," I whined.

"Get going, sweetie."

We followed my mom through the house to her back office full of paints and artwork and my father's storage cabinet.

She crossed her arms. "Every speck of paint needs to be peeled off the floor."

"Murë!"

"No magic," she added.

"What if it's a stain?"

"This isn't your mother's workshop, Nolan. The floor doesn't stain."

"But—"

"If there is a stain, you may leave it. I will check when you're done."

My mom never manually peeled her paint off her workroom floor. She gave us two brushes, a pail of hot soapy water, and two sharp blades for us to pick off the stubborn flakes.

"This is degrading, Murë. For something we didn't even do."

"Stop telling so many lies that I can't tell the truth from fiction."

"This is so unfair."

"I'll be in the kitchen, so don't even try using magic. I'll know." She always did, somehow.

Nol chose a brush and picked a corner. "Let's get this done, Hallë. We'll go to my house afterward."

"No, Raj and I are studying tonight."

"Oh..."

"I thought you had plans."

"I...did but—" He pressed his brush into the floor, fighting a war with the paint.

"But what?"

"It fell through."

"Oh."

I waited for a while, letting him sulk until he decided to tell me of these plans he spoke of, but he continued to scrub. Stop. Scrub. Pry at a piece of paint with the knife. Scrub again.

"Are you going to help?"

I grumbled and got to work. "Did these plans involve Jemi and Enyco?"

A few moments passed. "No."

Interesting. "Lahiem and Carena?"

"No."

I sat back on my heels and looked over at him scrubbing away. The tips of his ears, above his five looped ear cuff of his fifth decade honors—a decade early—were red.

"The girl?"

He stopped scrubbing. "I don't want to talk about it."

"Did you—did she—"

"I said, I don't want to talk about it."

"That's what you had going on? Why didn't you tell me? Can I go kick her ass?"

"Don't say ass here or Tiaë will kick yours. And no, you can't, you don't even know what she looks like."

I stuck my tongue out at him, but he didn't see.

"I didn't want to go in the first place."

"Then—"

"Gil set it up."

"Oh." We scrubbed in silence for a while.

"So, since you're not busy anymore, you could come help Raj and me."

He sat on his heels like me and frowned. "Hallë, I know you want us to be friends with her, but honestly, I don't feel comfortable around her."

I stared at him as he began scrubbing again. Did Raj see this? No, she told me before, Nol's future was muddied because of our bond.

Nol glanced up at me, then stopped cleaning. "What?"

"That's what Raj said you'd say."

"See?"

"No, I mean, she says everyone says that about her. It's hard for her to make friends."

"We've agreed that having other friends outside our circle is important."

"Yes, but that's not what I mean."

He continued, ignoring me. "And bringing a new friend into our circle will—"

"I know, but am I really asking that much from you? Getting to know her a little? I know your friends. I don't spend much time with them, I leave that up to you, but I know them. I didn't try to make Lahiem and Carena my friends."

"You don't leave that up to me. You always complain that I don't take you with me."

"It's been hard for me to let you go off on your own. Perhaps I am a little jealous, but only because you treat me like a little kid when you're around other friends."

"You are younger than all of us."

"I'm only nine years younger than you. Jemi and Enyco are almost one fifty. Do they even have plans after secondary school?"

He pointed his brush at me. "Do you want to know the real reason I've tried to avoid this? I know it will hurt you, but do you want to know?"

I dropped my brush and leaned back. "Sure."

He shook his hair out of his eyes. "You must always draw attention to yourself."

"Excuse me?"

"They don't enjoy going to events with you because you want all of my attention."

"I do not..." But then I thought about the times we went places together. "I don't mean to."

"Yes, you do. You just have no forethought of your actions."

I went back to scrubbing while I reflected on those few times.

"Don't pout."

"I'm not, I'm thinking. Do I do that with Gil, too?"

He tipped his head to the side, thinking. "Gil's different. You and I have always been together. I understand it's hard. If you are going"—he looked around and lowered his voice—"to *Pequwyn*, you'll need to learn to do without me."

Stunned, I rocked back and almost fell. "You're lecturing me on change?"

He tried to hide his smile. "*Pilassa.*" *Shut up.* "I know. We both have issues."

"Is that why Lahiem and Carena pull pranks on us? Because I tried to draw your attention away?"

He tossed his brush in the air, but it slipped through his fingers and clattered on the floor. "No, that's all in good fun. Truly. They keep pestering me about how we'll get them back."

"Let them stew."

We laughed, got back to work, and threw around prank ideas.

"Hey, brats." An'di stepped into the room sometime later. Her bright red hair was in a tangle, which I doubt started out that way. She hated her hair—I loved it. I loved Nol's, too. To have any red toned mop was better than my curly black hair.

Nol scowled and flipped his hair back, wet from his habit of shoving it out of his face. "What do you want, An'di?"

"Müre needs your help out in the yard. Nevie, your talent would be most appreciated."

"Um..." Wennië knew about our punishment, though. "We're not done with the floor."

She flicked her fingers out and winked. "You could be."

"No magic. My murë will know."

An'di rolled her eyes. "Tiaë! Murë needs Nevie's and Nolan's help. Can Nevie finish this up real quick?"

My mom's soft steps shuffled through the house. She walked in, a rag in her hands as she inspected our work. "Very well."

Nol threw his brush in the bucket and popped up. I still couldn't believe my ears.

"This doesn't mean all is forgiven."

"I know." My head bobbed, but my brain was still processing.

She lifted her chin, nodded once, and left.

"Let's go, Hallë," Nol hissed. "Any yard work is better than splinters under my fingernails."

I spread my magic wide and pictured the paint peeling under my knife. Every speck of paint lifted and incinerated. The bucket's water evaporated and floated out the window. I called Nol's knife, still in his pocket, and placed his and mine on my mother's worktable.

"Hallanevaë!"

"Sorry!" I'd also cleaned her floors throughout the house. Why not? She'd let us go—I was being nice.

"Magic is not for convenience, young lady."

"Laro?" I stuck my head in my dad's work room. "Raj and I are studying at the library tonight. It might go late. Talk to Murë for me?"

"Yes. Go on, sweetie. Tell Raj hello."

I kissed my dad's cheek and ran. Waiting for me at the door, Nol and An'di snickered at my annoyed look.

"You'd think she'd be grateful. Only my murë." We jogged to the *hassop* tree before stopping to talk. "What's Wennië wanting done?"

"Nothing. Just thought you'd had enough punishment for not doing much at all."

Without thinking, I flung my arms around her. "You are the best!"

"I know. I also know Nolan has something planned tonight." She wiggled her eyebrows.

"No. That isn't happening now."

"You sure? Because someone at our house says otherwise."

"What?" We jogged behind the *hossap* tree to peek through the orange-and-clove scented *murya* tree in their yard.

A light blond *endaë* with a light brown oval face and perfect nose stood on their stoop, looking out into the street. She kept her arms crossed and her thumbnail in her mouth. She looked nothing like Raj, except the hair. Raj's frame was daintier, with narrower shoulders, and not as tall—she'd fit right under Nol's arm.

This *endaë* stood at An'di's height, which meant tall enough to rest her chin on Nol's shoulder. Even biting her nail, she looked sophisticated with her long neck and squared shoulders. They'd look perfect together. My lip rolled up as I squinted at the pretty girl.

"Is that—Jespine?"

"Shut it."

"No wonder why you couldn't form a sentence in front of her," I teased.

"Could, too. I don't know about this."

"You'll be fine, little brother. Go make friends with the pretty girl." An'di shoved Nol past the tree. Startled, Jespine jumped back and almost hit the side of the house.

"Will he be all right?" I whispered, and remembered the words Nol told me, reminding myself not to be jealous of his new friends. Well, girlfriend. Possible, girlfriend. But not Rajamë.

"Sure, I'm sure. You're not jealous—"

"No. There's a girl who likes him, and I hoped that I could draw his attention toward her."

"Did you say something about it to him?"

"No, she asked me not to. She's shy."

"That pretty girl who you've made friends with? Rajamë? She's your age?"

"One thirty-three, but we're in the same classes. Except magical studies." I growled at my shortcomings. "Please don't tell anyone about Raj. She's so shy."

"What's the gossip on Jespine?"

"Prettiest girl in the school and she knows it. She's Nol's age but got her fourth honors two years ago—maybe three. I've never seen her take interest in Nol before."

"This won't last long then. Let The Mother take the reins."

I nodded. "I'm not going to tell Raj about this."

"Good idea. Come on."

"Where?"

"I've got a bit of shopping to do."

"And you want me to go with you?" She never spent time with me if she could avoid it.

"Sure, I thought you'd enjoy some sister time."

"I have to meet Raj at the library at sunset."

An'di shrugged. "We've got time, and the shop is closer to the library than here."

I took one last look at my *muranildo* with Jespine and shoved my worry down.

"I'd like that."

An'di took my hand, and we dashed out, giggling when they noticed us. Like we'd been stealthy at all.

6

"So what are we getting?"

"A few herbs and *merili*."

"For what?"

"Spells." An'di tugged on my hair and pulled me under her arm. "You sure are nosy."

"Do you have to leave tomorrow?"

An'di sighed. "Yes. You're starting to sound like my brother."

"I'm going to miss you."

"You mean, you're going to miss pestering me."

I beamed up at her from under her arm. "Out of love."

An'di scoffed and let me go.

"Murë doesn't let me go in here." I stood in front of Metina's Shop of Herbs and Trinkets. Although, my mom got lots more things in there than trinkets, but she never got herbs.

"I know." An'di shrugged and opened the door for me. "It'll be fine."

Metina would kick me out seconds after I walked through her door, but An'di insisted. She'd see.

"Hello," Metina greeted her new customers from the depths of her overstuffed store. Dried herbs and the tangy scent of *hossap* leaves burning threatened to make me sneeze. Colorful sashes clung to the ceiling, whether with nails or spell, I couldn't tell. Light filtered through the sashes from the windows above them. So the rainbow of colors that people saw in the windows came from that? Boring.

"Metina! It's me, An'di. Did it come in?"

Metina came out from behind a curtain; little bells connected to the fabric jingled as she pushed the curtain out of the way. Her skirt, really a bunch of old patches of sashes from above, swayed near her feet. The purple and green stains on her white blouse covered most of her sleeves and collar. Metina kept her hair partially pulled back into a bun, and the rest went everywhere.

"Oh, yes, it's here, and so is the *merili* amber. Come into the back." Her face fell when she saw me beside An'di. She crossed her arms and glared. Her bush of hair didn't even move when she tipped her chin. "Break anything, and you'll be washing the bird poop off my windows." She pointed to the sashes above.

I turned a slow circle. The junk in here wasn't worth keeping, but I bit my tongue. The decent items my mother got must be in the "back." The two *endai* stared down at me, waiting for a reply. "Yes, Metina." I sighed and followed them.

"I'm so glad it came before I left. I broke my last one yesterday and I needed to make a few potions to take with us."

"Oh good. Also, I'm packing Zella's new *meril*."

My ears perked up at my grandmother's name.

"Yalu? What *meril* does she need?"

"Oh." Metina looked up from the box of papers she had her hands in. "For her headaches. She lost the last one."

"That's Yalu," I mumbled, rolling my eyes.

As their conversation continued about An'di's infused herbs and healing spells, my attention drifted to the products on the shelves. An orange rock, a leather notebook, and a bottle of green liquid all sat together on a table.

"Nevie, leave that alone, please. They all belong to someone. If you're careful, you may go look at the notebooks in front. Nothing out there belongs to anyone."

"Okay. Can I have something?"

The two narrowed their eyes.

"Never mind," I muttered.

"If you're good, I'll get one thing, all right?"

"Yeah?" Why was An'di being so nice to me?

"You have to be good."

"I can do that."

Metina scoffed into her hand. Ignoring her instead of sticking my tongue out, I swished my hair back as I turned. They never believed in me; when I behaved, no one acknowledged it. But I sure got scolded a lot. When I had kids, I'd give them a lot more praise. I'd tell them how well they did and encourage them when they got off track. I hated it here.

Either Metina lied or didn't know her store very well because there were no notebooks in the whole disorganized mess. Books were haphazardly piled next to incense. Oils in glass bottles were precariously balanced on the edges of shelves, ready to fall right on top of colorful powders and white lace tablecloths. Would she mind if I reorganized a few things?

"Hey." An'di appeared beside me as I tried to read the label on a leather pouch.

"*Urro!*" I swore. "Don't scare me like that." I lowered my voice. "I don't want to be blamed for knocking all this over and have to clean her windows because she can't organize anything in here."

"Yeah, it's a bit much, huh?"

"A bit? No wonder Murë never lets me come in here. I turn wrong and a shelf of bottles will crash to the floor."

She shrugged. "What did you find?"

"No clue. I can't read her handwriting."

"What are you looking for?"

"Prank ideas."

"Ah." An'di picked up a little pouch and squinted at the label. "Here." She tossed it to me.

"*Ai*, be careful! I'm actually trying."

"It's potions this season, right?"

"Yeah?"

"This turns liquids purple and gooey. Throw some in and see what happens."

"That's horrid. Even I won't ruin their entire quarter's worth of work."

She shrugged. "Put it in their tea."

"That's childish."

"You are a child." An'di plucked it out of my hand. "Use it as a backup."

"You're horrible at pranks." But I let her take it to the front counter. "Thanks," I mumbled as Metina handed me the powder.

"I'll bring you the ointments when I get back," An'di assured her as she stuffed everything into her bag. "Anything else?"

"I need some of Wennië's blue dye, too. I'm sure she will need something in here for it."

"Do you have a bottle or do you need a new one?"

Metina frowned.

"New one, got it."

When we walked out, the sun was past the horizon. "How did we spend so much time in there? I have to go. Thank you, An'di." I bounced on my toes. "For taking me and...this." I shook the little pouch.

"Don't I get a hug? You won't see me for days."

I rolled my eyes but gave her a quick hug anyway.

"Rajamë!" I waved to her, then picked up my pace until I made it up the stairs of the Hall of Knowledge, out of breath. "I'm... here."

"Let's get working. Laro wants me home in an hour."

"In an hour? I thought we had an hour to study?"

She pursed her lips to keep from apologizing. She did that too much. It wasn't her fault her dad would rather her quit school.

"It's okay, we'll make the best of it. Come on."

We found a place at a far table on the second floor and pulled our books out as fast as we could. We both hated math but needed to get high marks. If we did well in this course, we wouldn't have to take another one—ever. Unless...

"What's wrong?" Raj asked when I paused.

"I don't know for sure. I need to ask Professor Hanno and Professor Baslen about math requirements for the apprenticeship. They're talking about going much earlier than one hundred fifty."

"But won't that mess everything up? Did you tell anyone?"

"Nol. I can't keep anything from him—"

"You didn't tell him about the international opportunity."

"Because it wasn't a sure thing. I told him yesterday, though."

We needed to study. I found the one problem in particular I needed help with. "Here, I'm not getting the answer right. It's off no matter what."

"Oh!" Raj perked up and showed me her notes from a day I'd skipped class with Nol, but he'd promised to teach me what they had discussed in class. I was still waiting.

The bell struck the hour and we both shot up, not realizing how fast time had passed.

"Laro is going to be so mad." Raj shoved everything into her bag; if she took any of my things, it didn't matter. We'd see each other tomorrow. "I'm just going to run ahead."

"I can come and tell him it was my fault." I couldn't stand her father. That *endao* had issues, but if it spared her, I'd play nice.

"No, that's okay. I'm only a few minutes from here. I thought you were going to research some spells for your prank."

My hand went to my shirt pocket with my new powder inside. I looked around at all these books, spelled lamps glowing at the end of every bookshelf. Where did Nol take his date, I wondered? Not here; at least, he better not have.

"I should."

"You don't seem so excited."

"I...I am. Go. We'll talk later."

Raj tucked her pack in close and walked, just under what the librarian would consider running. She waved to me before heading down the stairs.

The closest bookshelf to our table held all sorts of boring properties of natural magic. A book on how to make a *meril*. That might come in handy. I pulled that off the shelf and slid it next to my math book. Not that I needed a *meril* for anything at the moment. *Endai* made *merili* for communication, pain, traveling, and thousands of other reasons I couldn't name.

The next row over started the potions section. I touched my pocket again. "A sign, maybe?"

At the top, three shelves above my head, there was a gap, about three of my fingers wide. None of the surrounding books leaned in, so that meant a book. I liked short, squat books—just like me. I dragged my chair over, the loud scrape of wood over stone echoing through the library. Oh well, not many were here at this hour anyway. I stretched as far as I could, but even on the chair, my fingers were just able to brush the books on the top shelf.

I couldn't see the book from this angle, so even if I tried calling it to me, all the books on the shelf could come with it. Touching the two books on either side of the one I wanted, my magic nudged the middle one toward my palm. Inch by inch, the book slid closer. At last, it came into my view: worn leather, stained a deep wine red with gold lettering—well, what was left of it.

"Looks like you need to grow some more, freak."

"Leave me alone, Jemi." I dropped my arms and looked for him.

"What are you doing up here all alone?" He pressed on a few book spines as he walked closer. "Aren't you scared by yourself?"

Sighing, I jumped off the chair and backed up. "The question is, what are you doing in here? Did you get lost? I understand. The library is hard to navigate for newcomers like yourself."

"*Tuma juväe, Nevie,*" Jemi swore at me. "I heard how you cussed Rassel out in front of everyone."

I snorted. "Yeah, that's exactly how it went."

"Rumor has it that you'll be suspended. Again."

I crossed my arms and leaned against the bookshelf. "You're wasting my time. What do you want?"

"You went and whined to Nolan, and he wouldn't talk to us today."

"And?"

"We told you what would happen if you bitched to him."

Tiny pricks of pain cut my palms, startling me. I loosened my clenched fists. As I checked my palms for cuts, Jemi moved toward me.

"Stop, Jemi."

"Who's going to make me?" He reached for my head, but I ducked. He tried to snatch at me again, but I charged forward, into his lower abdomen. Jemi fell back onto his butt, shock in his eyes. I was pretty shocked myself. A head shorter than everyone else, fighting wasn't one of my talents.

"I am." I smirked to irritate him.

"You little bitch." Jemi scrambled to get to me and almost fell. I backed up, but the corner of the table rammed into my spine. Jemi kept coming, even as I fell into Raj's vacant chair. The table corner jabbed him right below his abdomen. I thought he'd yell, but he couldn't get any air. Everything was silent as his eyes bulged and both his hands went to his crotch. If I cared even a little about him, I'd have asked if he was all right. Call me heartless.

"Serves you right, you jerk." I grabbed my math book with two hands and smashed it into his shoulder. That's when he howled. I covered my ears and backed away. The librarian was going to kill me. She was one of the few who actually liked me in this city, and now she'd hate me.

"*Urro! Pilassa, Jemi.*" *Shut up, Jemi.* I shoved on him as he continued to howl, tears—yes, tears—streaming down his face. Growling at him for not shutting up and crying like a baby, I shoved the *meril* book and math book into my bag. I was getting out of here. Now. I was not getting blamed for this. Not caring if the other books fell now, I called the red book to me. The worn leather bound pages had more heft to them than I'd thought they would. I pressed the book against my chest and ducked out of the library as fast as I could. Jemi was still howling as I ran out the door.

7

"Nevie? Are you making all that noise?"

I took a deep breath, heart still pounding, as I leaned against the front door that I'd just slammed shut.

"Uh, sorry, Murë. I fell against the door, and it slammed shut."

"Are you all right?" My dad's voice came from the same direction as my mom's.

"Yep, everything is fine."

"Well, I'm glad you made your curfew tonight," Murë said in a way that made me think I hadn't. I didn't question it.

"Sure." Why were they acting so weird? "I'm getting ready for bed now. Night." I bolted up the stairs and away from my parents.

My room was at the end, upstairs, next to an old *murya* tree, like the one in Nol's yard. I flung open the door and threw my bag and books onto the bed. If I made my curfew, Nol wouldn't be here for an hour. Unless his date kept him out later. I smiled. While she wasn't Raj, I could finally start getting him back for all the comments he'd made about Gileal and me.

Excited to read this mystery book, I hurried to get dressed in my night clothes. Once on the bed, I pulled the book into my lap. *Urro*, the light. *Endai* had great night vision, but it only went so far. I conjured a light in the sconce on my wall.

My hand almost covered the front of the little red book, but the width took up most of my palm. The words on the front were in worse shape than on the binding. It smelled of old books and dust, like I'd expected. The angled letters and wispy tails suggested the book was written early last century, but the delicate pages suggested something even older…maybe two centuries?

The contents page numbered over a thousand spells, understandable considering the width. Although, did it give enough detail for me to use them? Most people could repeat the incantation and get the results, like a mathematical equation. Insert this word here plus this hand placement there equals light. I needed to know the how and the why. And I wasn't good at math.

"Evaporating potion?" I whispered. "I did that with the bucket of water today."

As gentle as possible, I flipped to the page and scrolled through the tiny words. My shoulders dropped. Words, incantations, and the specific hand movements for heat. A warning of how hot steam was, as if it could be anything but boiling hot. But the timing was controllable.

"How?" I whispered to the book. I kept scanning. "Dissolvable crystals?" Sure enough, using an infused dissolvable crystal would delay the reaction until it completely dissolved. Now, how did I infuse crystals? An'di infused her spells in her herbal teas and *merili*. I tossed the book across my bed and picked up the *meril* book. "This could work!"

"What could work?" Nol lifted himself over the window ledge.

"How was your date?"

Nol grumbled something.

"Speak up, I couldn't hear that."

"I don't like dating."

"Oh, come on, it couldn't be that bad."

"She expected me to kiss her. When was the first time Gil and you kissed? Did you instigate—"

"Okay, we're not getting into that. We're *muranildi*, but no way am I getting that personal. Did you kiss her?"

"No! I walked her home and when she asked if I was going to kiss her, I froze. *Ai*, Hallë! Then, when I told her no, she pouted—she pouts better than you!"

"I don't pout."

He met my smile with a flat glare. All right, so I pouted.

"Well, did she storm off?"

He scoffed. "She proceeded to list every part of our date where I failed."

"No."

"Yes. I don't want to date, I want to study. At least I don't fail at that."

"So you're mad that you failed dating."

"Yes—no, I don't know."

"But that's not all." Again, I made it a statement.

"Correct. Dating will distract me from my studies."

"Or you need to find someone who's as addicted to studying as you."

He scowled. "I'm not addicted to—"

"Then what would you call it? Failing at something isn't bad, it's a learning experience."

"I know that."

"You don't fail often. I'm sorry Gileal pushed you. Do you want me to talk to him?"

"No, I'll do it." He plopped on the bed beside me, plucking up the old book just before he fell on it. "So, what might work?"

"Huh?"

"What you said earlier. What do you have your nose in now?"

"Oh! After Raj had to leave, I found a few books. This one is how to make *merili*." I gave him the book, but he already had the other one in front of him. He lay on his side, his arm propping his head up, with the book on the bed. He flipped through the delicate pages quicker than me.

"This is old," he mumbled. "That could be a problem."

"Why?"

"Harder to recognize in case something goes wrong. You'll need to be certain—" He paused, his finger at the end of the contents page.

"What?"

"Don't use this book."

"Why?"

"I recognize this name. She's a *Mellorian* author."

"So? They're not bad people, we just don't get along with them right now. They were our allies in the past—"

"We've studied her methods in class. She wasn't a good person, Hallë. She created spells of great destruction, helped begin the war in the time of Sarcaerin."

"The Sarcaerin Era was eons ago, Nol. This book can't be older than two hundred years."

Nol's eyebrow ticked at my exaggeration of years. "Queen Sarcaerin died"—he looked at the ceiling, counting in his head—"three thousand, one hundred, thirty-nine years ago. My great-grandmother was alive when Queen Sarcaerin died."

"Well, put that way..."

"Regardless, this is also in *Aemirin*. Someone had to have translated it. Where did you get this book?"

"Where do you think? In the library."

"Where in the library?"

"The potions section, on the top shelf."

"The outside is worn, but not frayed. No one has read this in a long time. It doesn't have a library marking on it either. Someone put it in there."

"Well—" What was my point again? "Well, those spells aren't evil, Nol. Maybe she wrote this before her decline of morality."

He huffed. "What a great way of putting it."

"Look, the spell I found just evaporates water on a controlled time."

"What do you mean?"

"You infuse a dissolvable crystal—"

"Ah, I see." He read the spell and warnings ahead of my explanation. "It doesn't seem too bad, but it doesn't have a lot of description here. How would you infuse the crystal?"

"That's why I was looking at the *meril* book."

"*Meril*?"

"Yes, this. An'di does it all the time with her teas and medicines. And that's how *merili* are made. See?"

Nol snatched the book I waved in his face. "There are reasons why everyone doesn't make *merili*, Hallë." He took a breath, dropped the book on the bed, and spun it around. "See here? You must destroy the *meril* if it doesn't set right."

"So?"

"*Merili* have the potential of imploding if the seam is—"

"I can read it, Nol. You don't have to recite it for me."

I hated it when he did that. He remembered everything. Nol's father, Edvic, had said Nol's retention and comprehension placed him in a small percentile of individuals. Put simply, Nol was a genius. Usually, he didn't gloat or show off, but he was being a jerk.

"We'll find another spell for the prank. Plus, it doesn't have enough description for you to interpret it for your own magic."

"I can do it traditionally, then."

"No. Your control isn't good enough yet."

"I've gotten better."

"Yes, but it's an advanced spell. Things could go wrong."

"How is it advanced? The instructions are simple. You're just making up excuses because you don't think I can do it."

"I'm not making excuses. And no, you can't do it. We're not using it."

"Because our history books consider this person evil?"

"Yes."

"Do you think every *Mellorin* is inherently bad, then?"

"No, but she made spells to kill people, *Aeminan* citizens. We're not using this."

This was my *muranildo*, telling me I wasn't good enough. He'd seen my progress. I'd always trusted him and respected him, but... "Fine. You need to find something then, I'm tired of looking."

"It's your turn to look, plus, I'm busy. Like you said earlier, let them stew. You'll find something, you're Hallanevaë, the most powerful *enda* in the world."

I scoffed. "That is so not true."

"You might be. Your grandparents are powerful *endai*, your father is just as powerful—on a different spectrum. It is only logical that you are even more powerful."

"Shut up. I don't want to hear it from you, too."

He poked me. "They'll test you once your magic shows signs of leveling out. Then those professors will eat their words."

"I don't want to be tested."

"The *Amura Ore* will insist on it."

I groaned and lay across from him, mirroring his position.

He poked me again. "I'm sorry for making you mad."

I wrinkled my nose and he thumped it.

"Stop that," I growled and covered my nose.

"Why? You look so cute when your face scrunches up like that."

"*Ai*, cute is for babies. I'm not cute or adorable."

"Fine, you're becoming a beau–"

"Don't!" I shoved him. "You're such a liar and I don't want to hear such crap from you."

He laughed as I kept shoving him. Nol got a poke every time he tried to say it. He tried grabbing my arms but wasn't strong enough to hold me down. When he fell off the end of the bed, we paused, our eyes wide, and then we both laughed.

My dad came in while I was trying to right my covers around Nol, who had his feet propped up against the end of the bed.

"Laro?" I pushed my hair out of my face and waited to see what he had to say.

"You two all right in here?"

"Nol's just being his klutzy self."

"And making her mad."

"That's not hard to do," my father grumbled.

"Tell her she's adorable when she's mad."

"Twynolan, I swear I'll beat you with this pillow and send you home!" I held the pillow above my head as he continued chuckling. "Laro! Make him stop."

My dad stared between the two of us. "He's your *muranildo*, if you haven't gotten control of him by now, you never will. Anyway, you two, it's time to settle down. Nolan, if you can't keep quiet, I'll have to send you home."

Nol cleared his throat and took his feet off the bed. "Yes, Orin."

"Did you both clean your teeth?"

Nol groaned and went to our bathroom.

"He was out on a date tonight," I explained while tidying up my room.

"Oh? With whom?"

"Jespine, but it didn't go well. Poor guy doesn't know the first thing about girls."

"Well, you're a girl, and he knows how to get along with you."

"Right, like gender is important in our relationship. I doubt he even realized I was a girl until he was fifty, maybe older."

"That's not true. I think he was closer to twenty, actually. When he saw An'di style your hair with some flowers."

"What about Hallë's hair?"

"When you realized Nevie was a girl."

"Oh, I've always known you're a girl—I just never held it against you."

I threw my pillow at him as he ducked behind my father, both of them smiling.

"Orinzelis! What is going on up there? Tell your daughter and Nolan to get to bed and come help me."

"Oh, she got your whole name in there, Laro. She's ticked."

"A bit." My dad came all the way in and kissed my forehead. "Be nice to him, he's the only one you've got."

Nol gave me a goofy grin and stuck his tongue out at me.

"And she's the only one you've got." Dad pulled him in for a hug. Nol was almost a head taller than him now, I realized. "You may both have your friends, but the two of you will be beside each other until the end. Make it a pleasant twelve hundred years."

I rolled my eyes and got into bed. Nol pounced in right after the door closed. With a flick of his fingers, Nol snuffed out the light. He settled in, touched his cold feet to mine before he adjusted his blankets, then again and a third time.

"Twynolan, what is going on? Stop wiggling."

"I can't get comfortable." He wiggled a bit more and elbowed me in the process.

"*Ai*, you are about to be kicked off the bed."

"Oh?" He reached over and tickled me.

My knee hit his hip as I tried to get my legs in to shove him off the bed. He realized my intention, got up on his knees, and sat on me before I could kick him. All while tickling me.

"Okay! Okay, you win. Stop!"

He kept going.

"Nol! I promise—"

He stopped. "What?"

"I promise...not to kick you out...of the bed."

"Better." He got off and lay down again. "Now go to sleep, we've got lessons in the morning."

Scoffing, I rolled away and worked to calm my breathing.

"Hallë?" Nol said after a while.

"Hmm?" Sleep would come soon, and I didn't want to talk.

"So we agree, right?"

"Hmm?"

"About the book and the spell?"

"Mmmhmm. You want to find something else. Go to sleep."

"All right, but I mean it."

COMPLETE DARKNESS SWALLOWED ME. My body felt weighted down and cold. So cold. The plunk of a drip of water falling into a pool came from my right. Another drop and a splash. I lifted my hand to conjure a light orb, but nothing came. The floor fell out from under me, but I didn't fall. My hair and clothes pulled me down, and I was underwater somehow.

No breath, so cold. My feet wouldn't kick—they were getting caught up in the dress I wore. Something hit my side, and then something hit my other side. I screamed underwater, but no sound came out. Something hit my stomach and I kicked enough to reach the surface and breathe.

I searched for something to hold on to, fumbling in the dark. A hand gripped my wrist. It had long thin fingers, too long to be *endaen*. It clamped its fingers around my hand, pressing and sliding into my skin. I tried to scream, but it pulled me under again. Water filled my lungs.

Warmth spread from my core; a light of some sort came from underneath me. The thing released me and swam off, not letting me get a glimpse of it. The surrounding light lifted me out of the water, where a shore appeared. Between one blink and the next, the warm light dried my clothes and hair. I could breathe and I settled.

My eyes fluttered open. The room was silent, other than the sound of the frogs chirping outside. The moon glowed silver on the other half of my room. Nol's arm rested over my back, his head against my shoulder.

"Are you all right?" he whispered.

I rolled over until our foreheads touched. "Yeah. Did you see what it was?"

"You don't want to see it, Hallë. Thank the Mother, the creatures your mind invents aren't real."

"Will you be able to sleep now?"

He paused. "I will be fine. Go to sleep. We'll keep our bond open the rest of the night."

"I'm sorry."

He lifted his head, his pale blue eyes glowing almost silver in the moonlight. "Never apologize for your nightmares. They're not your fault. Go to sleep and I'll follow soon after."

I sniffled and nodded. A thought, or a feeling deep in the back of my mind, held on to the part of me that wasn't Hallanevaë. I found the warmth next to it that wasn't Twynolan, but his soul, and we held each other close. If I dreamt again, I didn't remember.

8

"*C'yo!*" I muttered when my quartz cracked for the third time.

"Better not let your parents hear you swearing like that," Lahiem said from her desk, where she worked on...whatever apprentices worked on while she babysat me for my noon detention. Well, almost apprentice. As soon as she turned one hundred fifty she would start her apprenticeship here under Professor Asin.

I whispered the spell and performed the small hand motion again, and my fourth quartz broke. I didn't want to ask for more quartz, and I was running low.

"Let me help—"

"No, I need to figure this out. It's the only one I haven't figured out for the midterm today."

"Humor me."

I dropped my hands. "Ugh. Fine."

She laughed at my annoyance like she was so much older than me.

"What are you working on?" She pulled my book over to her. Lahiem's eyebrows went high. She'd tried to hide her reaction, but I'd caught it.

I bit my lip. "I know, but this one seemed easy, so I decided to come back to it."

"Thermal conductivity is not easy, Nevie."

"It's just heating some quartz up. I can do that on my own."

"Using your magic doesn't count. Show me how you're doing it the traditional way."

I placed some quartz on the hot dish and allowed enough of my energy to flow through while I drew the symbols in the air and said the incantation. "*Hata sama tenasos quole.*"

And…the dish began to shift colors as the quartz got hotter. Then…the quartz cracked. "*Urro*! I'm never going to get this." I laid my head on the table and stared at the darkening dish.

"You need to stop thinking so much."

"Asin says we need to focus and have intent."

"You have enough intent for the entire school. When you start this spell, or any of these"—she tapped my textbook—"what are you thinking of?"

"The same thing as everyone else—what I want it to do."

"But you're not like everyone else. Your thoughts propel your magic forward, while other *endai* use words and motions. When you cast traditional spells, you use both."

"How do you know that?"

"Nolan and I talk."

"Of course you do." I dropped my chin into my palm.

"Your magic is feeding the spell, compounding the energy…This is all just speculating." She pulled my book over and flipped back. "Try this. I want you to show me the hand movements for heat."

"Heat? That's first decade stuff."

"Fundamentals, we all go back there when we need them. Please try."

She sounded like Professor Asin. With another encouraging nod, I traced the simple symbol for heat in the air—an exact horizontal line to the right, with a forty-five degree angle down to the left.

"Good. Now show me"—she placed her hand on the page at random—"the placements for *serian tryenun abe.*"

"*Tryenun* series? We're not doing manipulations yet." Still in the same category, though.

"I know you."

"Fine. I'd need to know the exact composition of quartz for that."

"Estimate. You're not invoking it."

"Is this going to be on the test?"

"Maybe."

"*Urro!*"

She gave me a sanguine smile, enjoying my frustration. "Try, Nevie."

I gritted my teeth as I concentrated. "The loop needs to be tight, and since I need to make it malleable, I need to curve up five degrees."

"You almost have it."

"I would touch the end of the horizontal and...cross down through the center to make sure the manipulation holds its shape when I'm done."

"Good. Now practice that a few times. You can talk it out here, but not when you're casting it."

"But you said I'm not doing it."

"Would you trust me?" She winked, stood up, and went back to her desk.

"Would you trust me," I mocked as I started the placements again. And again. Too many more times to count.

"Now, demonstrate the spell," she told me fifteen minutes later. She stopped beside me, stuffed her hands in her pockets, and rocked back on her heels. She'd be a great professor one day.

I took a breath to ground myself. "*Fida javet towea gansinde.*"

"What are you thinking when you say it?"

"Trying not to think, like you said—which is impossible."

"Focus on speaking. Don't think ahead."

I said it again, word for word.

"Perfect. Now show me the placements for your spell."

With a sigh, I focused on the words. "*Sama*"—right horizontal swipe—"*tenasos*"—negative forty degrees and loop around to cross the horizontal line to stabilize the heat.

"Isn't yours easier now that you've practiced the more complicated one?"

"Sure..."

"Now invoke it," Lahiem said, interrupting my thoughts.

"Ah..." It wasn't going to work. Not without intent.

"You can do this without their spell, right?"

"Easily."

"Then use that confidence in this spell."

"Astur." Okay. I planted my feet and wiggled the quartz on the dish. *"Hata, sama tenasos, quole."*

"There, look!" Lahiem called out, startling me.

"I did it?" Yes, the dish was white. "Yes! Lahiem, thank you so much." I hugged her tight but let go to watch the quartz. "I appreciate the time you took to help me study."

"You'll do fine on your test. Just don't overthink it. Confidence."

"Right." I shoved all my books into my bag, along with the spell An'di had bought me at Metina's.

"So...any warning for your prank?"

"You'll find out when it happens. Thank you again." I bolted down the hall.

"Nevie! No running," Jerric called out from his room.

No stopping. I had one more hall to go. The first student there got first selection on all the ingredients and equipment. I reached Asin's class, my feet slapping the floor, and I slowed to a halt three steps into the room. At my seat, I pulled out my books.

Giggling from the entrance brought my head around. Maisye and Fellë chattered on about boys—I think I heard Nol's name. Both girls giggled when I tipped my head their way.

"Nevie, I heard Nolan went on a date with Jespine last night," Maisye said.

"Stop gossiping, Maisye."

"You didn't know?" Fellë's smile dropped, and she stuck her lip out. "Oh, Nevie."

Maisye giggled. "He was probably too embarrassed. Jespine said he wasn't a good kisser, and he missed her face."

Maisye's and Fellë's faces darkened as they giggled.

I sneered. "Just remember, Maisye, there's always two sides to a story." And I'd be paying Jespine a visit tonight.

As the other students started filing in, Jemi knocked right into Fellë, but Maisye and I caught her before she fell.

"You're in the way," he barked.

"Or is it that you're incapable of going around anything? People, tables?" I wiggled my eyebrows.

Jemi's light taupe and amber eyes glowed with hatred. I covered my smile and rested my other hand on my lower stomach.

"It's going to cause irreparable damage one day," I taunted.

Jemi clenched his fists and bared his teeth. He took one step closer to me before Professor Asin walked through the door.

"We have a full schedule today. Take your seats without haste. Nevie, I need to see you in my office." Asin walked right past everyone without a backward glance.

The class erupted in gossip.

"Oh, what did she do this time?"

"Was she going to cheat?"

"Detention? Again?"

And it went on from there.

Ignoring their whispers as best I could, I hurried into Asin's office. "Yes?" I asked, trying to stay cheerful.

"How is your studying going?"

Oh no, he was going to do it again. "Lahiem helped me practice today. She says I'm ready."

"Good. I'm glad to hear you're working hard—and I see that. I do. I've noticed you struggling on a few spells that are on this test."

"Everyone does. If you don't struggle, there's no learning. Professor, you don't need to worry. I can do the spells."

He fidgeted with his shirt, unwilling to meet my eyes. "While that may be so, you know you become...unpredictable."

"But I've studied. I can do these—please let me show you."

"No, that's fine. I've decided to test you separately."

"Professor!"

"Nevie, listen, I've given this much thought. You'll only be demonstrating placements and preforming adjusted spells. Away from the others—it serves multiple purposes."

"Please, let me test with everyone."

"This is for everyone's safety, as a precaution. I don't like it when others pick on you for your disability."

I ground my teeth. "It's not a disability."

"Your erratic magic has interfered with your ability to perform simple spells, even though you know the placements and incantations. That's disabling your progress in your casting studies."

My tears started falling the moment he uttered erratic. "This isn't fair." Although, I wasn't sure if he'd understood me through my crying. "This isn't fair," I whispered a second time.

"No, it isn't—but I must insist. You will do these adjusted spells in a separate room today. Is that clear?"

I nodded at the paper he held up.

"This isn't your fault, Hallanevaë. Please understand this isn't a punishment."

"I can do all the spells you assigned in class." As of today, that was true, but he hadn't witnessed my success.

"You'll only demonstrate the placements. I'll be back soon. Sit, please, and wait for me."

I dropped to his chair. Asin gave me the paper as he left with a curt nod.

"These aren't the spell we've been practicing," I hissed. "These are for youngsters!"

Asin left the door open. He called for the class to settle down and get out their notes. Then after a few moments he came back in with his arms full. "Here is your equipment. You won't need much for this test."

"I've already worked on these placements and spells."

"It is always important to practice—and perfect—the fundamentals. No one is above these." His words rang similar to Lahiem's words earlier. Had she known Asin was going to do this?

"It's also good to provide challenges to determine one's boundaries."

He gave me a flat look after I quoted his own words. Most of the test was about symbols, placements, and math. He wanted to see two spells. Everyone else was performing fifty for their test. After half an hour, Asin came to check on my progress and found me waiting for him.

"Why aren't you working?"

"I'm done."

"Done?" He pulled the test off the table. "Good job getting those placement problems solved."

"I told you, I did this already. I wouldn't be in your class if I couldn't do these."

He shifted his weight and set the paper on a pile. "Cast the recharging energy spell—"

"Seriously? That is so lame." At his pointed look, I shut up and traced the "light" symbol and muttered the incantation. Electricity danced in the glass globe that he kept in his office for this very purpose. My core energy reached out and the spell ignited—exactly how it was supposed to.

"That's enough. Release it."

I glared at him and thought about making it glow brighter, but that would be proving his point. I released it. Asin pulled out a bottle of liquid, small enough to fit within his closed fist. He placed it on the table in front of me and backed up.

"Extract the salt out of the water through the cork."

I hated this one but did it regularly with my mom's paints. So much thought went into it. Why did traditional spells have to take so long? I centered myself, then cast the "separate" and "call" symbols and made sure I closed it off so the water stayed in the bottle. I muttered the incantation to call salt to my hand. A pinch of salt collected in my palm.

Asin knew I could do it. He called the bottle to him, opened the lid, and checked the salinity.

"Good. Go get your stuff."

"This is ridiculous," I muttered to myself as I left his office. What was the point of making me learn their spells if they didn't let me do them? I pulled out my chair to reach my bag under the desk.

"What's wrong, Nevie? Did you fail again?"

"*Pilassa, Esdeos.*" *Shut up, Esdeos.*

"You did fail!" Esdeos cackled. Everyone lifted their heads from their tests. I wanted to take his long sienna braids and choke him until his gray eyes bulged.

"So ironic. The girl with the most power can't even conjure simple spells. What was the Mother thinking?" Lorie said, a tall *endaë* with long creamy yellow curls, soft sepia skin, and smoky marine blue eyes. Why did I ever want to look like her?

"I can do spells just fine, Lorie."

"Prove it," she challenged.

Oh, now she was in for it. "Fine." The room went silent. I called the quartz on her table towards me, heated it with my own magic, and threw it back at her. She squeaked as the quartz levitated in the air a foot in front of her. "Keep talking and you'll see what I can really do." Her eyes didn't blink as she stared at the hot little thing, close enough that she could feel the heat but not close enough to hurt her.

"That's enough! Nevie, magic is not to be abused like this. Souloritaë." Asin turned, calling Lorie by her full name as he walked her way. "That was immature and shameful of you to antagonize her like that. You will know, Nevie completed and passed her exam. Early. I see you're not very far. One must ensure their flawlessness before correcting others. That goes for all of you. Nevie. My office. Now!"

I expelled the heat from Lorie's quartz and set it in my hand, room temperature once again. I walked over to her desk and placed it on the plate. She hadn't even finished her third calculation.

"Your calculation for *estua petenis* is wrong by a factor of two."

Lorie pinned me with a glare.

"Nevie!" Asin yelled.

I winked and jogged after Asin. Yes, I'd get in trouble, but damn it was worth it.

Once we were in the room, he closed the door and opened his outer door into the hallway. "Detention—two weeks. Do you realize how much danger you put Lorie in with that stunt?"

"None. It never would—"

"You will test in one week before lessons begin."

"What?"

"Until then make use of Lahiem's lab after school. Out!"

"Why do you hate me so much?" I yelled, turned, and ran out his door. If only I could drop the class—but I needed it to get into the *Aeminan* political program. I skipped my last two classes, too angry to focus on anything other than getting back at Professor Asin.

"I hate it here," I grumbled as I left the campus. "May the Mother toss them into The Starless Abyss." Instead of facing my parents, I crawled up Nol's ladder to my room.

"They never let me show them!" I paced my room as I vented. "Never challenge me. I have to prove to everyone I can do the spells."

I stopped at the end of my bed, where I'd pushed Nol off after he'd told me not to do the prank spell. That it was too advanced for me. Too risky. "Not even Nol believes in me." The book lay partially under my bed. "He doesn't think I'm capable of doing their spells." I sat on the floor and picked up the small old book with no name. "Well, I'm going to show all of them. They'll see. I'm just as good as they are."

9

I thumbed through the book until I found the spell. Since the book was *Mellorian*, many of the ingredients were native to that region, but I was sure there were equivalent substitutions here in *Aemina*. I'd do everything right and document it.

Metina should have all the ingredients I needed. Everyone was still in lessons, so I didn't have to worry about Nol. I used the window again—not to hide, but to prevent a conversation that would delay my work. I walked to Metina's, the chime going off as I entered. Metina called out from the back again. She had rose incense burning, inducing a grounding effect.

"Metina? It's Nevie." I went straight to the counter and waited. "I'm looking for some ingredients."

The tiny bells attached to the curtain separating the back tinkled as she swept them aside. "Nevie, just because I let you in here with An'di doesn't mean I'll let you come in whenever."

"Yes, but didn't I prove myself when I was in here? You have a lot of things precariously balanced over breakable, stainable items that would ruin everything under it. By the way, I'd be happy to help reorganize things to keep them safer. I'm good at that."

Metina pursed her lips and grew redder by the second as I offered my help. Oops.

"Because I enjoy doing that kind of stuff, and you seem busy."

"What do you need."

"I'm only looking for a few ingredients for my prank on Lahiem and Carena. I think I've found a great one. Please?"

"Lahiem's, I heard, was outstanding."

"That's an understatement. Nol and I've been looking for a while, but like I said, it's my turn."

Resigned, she sighed. "What are the ingredients?"

I bounced on my toes. "I'm looking for a dissolvable crystal. There's a few noted, but maybe you might know others." *That's right, Nevie, ask for her expertise.*

"Give me the names."

"*Calcisin, gosarsin,* and *melatersin.*"

"Hmm." She tapped her chin with her pencil. "Well, the *melatersin* you won't find outside of *Mellori. Gosarsin* I'm out of, it's an antiseptic, but I'll have that in the spring."

"And the *calcisin*?"

"Yes, I do have that. I'm assuming you'll be infusing a spell into this."

"How did you know?"

"Why do you think I have a shop? I'm a professional. You need to be careful, Nevie. This seems like an advanced spell."

"How so?"

"Infusing a spell into something is similar to making *merili*. Those are hard."

"Right, but—"

"You are an advanced student and Zella's granddaughter, I'm sure you'll find your own—safer—version. Anything else?"

"Oil."

"Ah yes, a sealant. *Remeso* oil will work well."

I'd never needed to use a sealant, but they were commonplace. "I think that's it."

"Normally, an infusion spell requires an essential oil of some sort—does yours have that?"

"Oh, let me check." I pulled the book out and kept the front covered. No need for her to get curious. "Um, *reafuraë*?" *Star blossom.*

"That's a rare one—another *Mellorian* item. Where did you find this spell?"

"The library. Do you have it?"

"No…but a good substitute is *astar*." *Moonflower.* "They're very close relatives."

"With the same properties?"

"Yes, most use *astar* because *reafuraë* isn't readily available now that we're not allies with *Mellori*."

"Okay, you're the expert."

"Professional, not expert." But she looked proud of my assessment. "Anything else?"

"How fast will this dissolve?"

"Mm, it's a ratio thing. Calculate the mass and use a one-two ratio."

"Then I'll only need a small amount. Thank you for the help. I want to do this right. I'm documenting everything."

"What is it?"

"Will you tell Carena or Lahiem?"

"I swear to secrecy."

I laughed. "It's not that serious. I'm going to swap their potions out with fake ones and evaporate them—but I need the crystal as a timer so it will start once they're in the room and I'm hiding."

"That makes sense, just be careful. These can get out of hand."

"I'll only use a little." If she was that serious, I would rather use too little and not dissolve the entire liquid.

She pulled out a fist-sized crystal of a beautiful blue that changed shades in the light. On one side, the crystal was teal blue, but on the other side it was a dusty blue. Then at another angle, it was as periwinkle blue as Raj's eyes. Light was such a fickle thing. Metina broke the crystal in half with her bare hand and wrapped it in a piece of paper.

"It's heavy for being so tiny and breakable," I said as she handed me the wrapped crystal.

"It's the metal in it." She handed me the oils in one of her cloth bags. "Good luck. And Nevie? After you invoke it, don't wait too long to use it. The sooner, the better. As the spell soaks in the crystal, it becomes more potent."

"I'm following all the instructions, no deviations. Promise!"

Out of breath from running across the town spiral and all the way into the science department, I shut the door of the smallest lab right before Professor Jerric and Professor Mejorë reached the laboratory hall, Mejorë laughing at another of Jerric's ridiculously childish jokes. All six workrooms were connected, but this one, at the very end of the dead-end hall, wasn't used for classes. But also, this little one was connected to Jerric's potions lab, and most importantly, where all the students stored their projects.

The oils needed to be stirred and activated the night before the crystal was charged to make sure the magic and oils were homogenized. That made sense. "Invoke the infusion no sooner than the morning of use." It advised a point five to two ratio. Even safer.

I added nine drops of *astar* essential oil in with the *remeso* oil. Conjuring a stirring spell, I let it spin while I went to check the weight of Carena's and Lahiem's potions. Potions, conveniently, needed to have all the information attached to the bowls.

I measured out the correct mass for all three pieces of crystal—one for each, plus a tester. Then I wrapped each one in a piece of paper so it didn't break on the walk home. Now to activate the infusion so they could homogenize.

"That's a ridiculously complicated way of putting it," I mumbled, reading the incantation. "Even for *Mellorian*." Then again, the book was old. Taking a breath to clear my mind, I traced the symbol and read the words, not worrying about what the *Mellorian* words meant or what it needed to do, just like Lahiem said. "*Fisac mayelinic cadaemes bomis letami tuca*." What a mouthful.

I felt nothing—no charge, no energy escalating in the oil. "*Savante*." I cast the canceling word, just in case. All the directions were followed, so why didn't it invoke? Even if my *Mellorian* was accented, it wouldn't matter. I cleared my mind again, repeated the incantation, and traced the symbol. Again, nothing. What was I doing wrong?

"*Savante*," I said, clearing it again. This was more advanced, according to Metina and Nol. I took a step back and looked at my surroundings. I knew what the incantation meant, as wordy as it was.

If I thought of the translated words, spoke them in *Mellorian* but thought them in *Acmirin*, perhaps my mind would understand? Would that be the same thing as using my magic? No. That was a language thing, nothing magical. I cleared my mind of everything, focusing only on this spell.

Thoughts away, a deep breath, and I traced the symbol...taking my time to get it exactly right while paying attention to the translation of each word. Not the spell. The magic ignited and the spell sealed. Finally. I measured out the correct amount of oil for each and hid it in the back of the shelf.

By the time everything was put away, night had fallen. My mom was going to kill me if I was too late. I checked on the time in the hall. Five minutes to curfew. I bolted and arrived home five minutes late.

"Murë," I called out as I got close and saw her form on the front steps. Five minutes and she was already waiting. "Sorry, I'm late. It took more time to clean up than I expected."

My mother stood on the front stoop with her arms crossed, her bright amethyst eyes glaring at me.

"Promise. Here's my lab book and the spell I was making. See?" I opened the bag and showed her. She didn't look. "I have to place the crystals in the moonlight to charge them before I can complete the spell, though."

"What?"

"To disperse the spell in the solution. The crystal dissolves."

"Is this a course project?"

"Uh...No. It's the prank I found for Lahiem and Carena."

"Oh, you found one, did you?"

It took me a few heartbeats to realize she was actually curious and not being sarcastic. "Yeah. Finally."

"You worked on it after lessons?"

"Yes. It's a traditional spell."

My mom stepped down until she was right in front of me and grabbed my shoulders. She leaned over until our noses touched. "You don't need to prove anything to them." Seconds passed until I thought that was all she was going to say. "But I've seen your frustration and struggle."

Wait—she was supporting me in this?

"Thanks, Murë." I jumped and surprised both of us when I wrapped my arms above her narrow shoulders. She was more than a bit taller than me. She teetered off balance, and we almost fell to the ground, but in a split second I had us stable.

"Don't let them define you, Nevie. Your magic is just as valid and worthy as theirs. I know what Professor Asin did today."

"How?"

"You've got this annoying *muranildo* who likes to take your side all the time. He's in there drinking tea with your laro, Wennië, and Edvic...although Edvic brought over his wine, so the fathers are a little tipsy."

"Nol?"

"*Ai*, no. He was just making fun of them." She put her arm around me and pulled me in the house. "But I'm not out here to scold you for being a few minutes late. Before you go in..." Anxiety tied my stomach in knots at her tone. "Not to scare you, but there was an incident today. I'll let Nolan tell you, but just so you understand, everyone is okay."

"He's hurt?"

My mom pulled on my shoulder to stop me from leaving her there. "He's just a bit scratched up. Wennië thinks he hit his head. Nolan isn't sure."

I'd been in a lab, messing around with a stupid prank, while Nol got hurt?

"Nevie. Nevie. Look at me." She held my face and forced me to look in her eyes. "He's fine. Please tell me you hear me before I let you go."

"He's—he's fine. He's fine."

"Nolan is in the kitchen with Wennië."

That was all I needed to know.

"Nol!" I ran through the house and into our large kitchen. Lights were cast everywhere, dishes in the basin, the window over the oven wide open, blowing on the herbs hanging from the ceiling, filling the kitchen with an herbal scent that smelled more like my grandmother's house. Wennië sat with Nol at the kitchen table, a healing kit next to the tea kettle. Nol held his tea; his palms and forearms were wrapped with bandages.

He stood as soon as he saw me.

"I'm okay." But he had his arms open, knowing it didn't matter what he said, I had to see for myself.

An instant later, I was in front of him, inspecting all his bandages and poking at the huge bruise on his cheekbone. He had a cut under his chin that I wasn't sure any of them knew about. He'd fallen, I was sure of it. He always fell, but this time it looked worse.

"What happened? Did you fall off the ladder? Down the stairs? It doesn't look like you broke anything this time."

Nol's eyebrow went high as he waited for me to stop talking.

"Well?" I encouraged.

"I'm all right."

"I see that. Now what happened."

Nol puffed his cheeks out and looked at his mom.

"Hi, Nevie." She sipped her tea like nothing was wrong. Like her son hadn't hurt himself. Again.

"Hi, Wennië."

She raised an eyebrow—the same one Nol unconsciously rose all the time. I groaned, leaned over, and kissed my second mom's cheek.

"He's fine, sweetie. We're taking care of it."

"Why won't anyone tell me?" My voice hitched at the end and Wennië gave in.

"Nolan, you should tell her before she starts panicking. Go ahead and go on up to bed. You've had three cups of tea now. I'm proud of you for finishing them."

Nol scowled and wiped his tongue on the roof of his mouth. "Night everyone." He waved at them all and pulled me out of the room and up the stairs, all the while silent. This wasn't a fall.

Nol sat on my bed when we got to my room.

"Enyco shoved me down on the way home and took my bag."

"What?" I couldn't breathe, and my heart thudded so loud I couldn't hear.

"Breathe, Hallë." He took my hand and tugged. "Breathe." I forced air into my lungs, watching his pale eyes stare pointedly at me until I inhaled a full breath.

"I thought—" I growled. "You were with Gileal."

"Yes, but they waited until we separated."

"This was premeditated. Was Jemi there?"

"No. He went for Gileal."

I gasped and had to sit beside him. "Is he okay?" They would have told me if something serious had happened. Wouldn't they? "Who knows?"

"My parents and your parents. Gil went to my house. He fought off Jemi and suspected Enyco had attacked me. I don't remember much from after Enyco left. Murë isn't sure if I have a concussion, so she wants me to take it easy."

"Did our parents go to theirs?"

"Tomorrow we're going to tell the headmaster."

"This isn't the school's responsibility. This should be a local council matter. They need to be charged with assault."

"That's what I think, too. Dad is concerned that it'll blow out of proportion, and we'll see what the headmaster's opinion is tomorrow, considering our course supplies were stolen. Including homework. Besides, with Zella gone, they're out their third member. No decisions can be made until she's back."

Technically, that wasn't true. They'd call in a proxy if emergency decisions needed to be decided. Something this small, though, wouldn't warrant much of their attention. Nol looked tired, or that could have been the bruise. Sleep would do him good.

"You need to sleep."

Nol got ready first—they'd brought his clothes. His parents, no doubt, would sleep here in their room downstairs.

I set the crystal on my dresser with some of my other trinkets so Nol wouldn't think much of it. He was already tucked against the wall and asleep when I got back with pajamas on and teeth cleaned.

10

Nᴏʟ ᴡᴀs sᴛɪʟʟ ᴀsʟᴇᴇᴘ when I woke up. While he wasn't a morning person, he usually woke before me. Tucking one hand under my cheek and facing him, I tugged on his hair. He didn't respond. I tugged again with the same conclusion.

"Nol, wake up, we have lessons." My voice was still heavy with sleep.

He stirred but didn't open his eyes. Not normal. Maybe Wennië's suspicion was right. I got up on my forearm and shook his shoulder.

"Mmm, headache...*sajat.*" *Quiet*, he mumbled.

I threw the covers off us and climbed out of my huge bed. Nol groaned and pulled the covers back over himself. It wouldn't hurt him to skip lessons, but he needed to be at the meeting. Wennië and my mom were at the kitchen table with toast and tea.

"Toast?" Wennië offered.

I nodded.

"Where's Nolan, sweetie?" My mom asked as Wennië set two pieces of bread on the oven for toasting. Wennië looked similar to Nol in coloring. Like the rest of her family, she had red hair, although hers was richer than her children's and as curly as mine. We always complained together. Her eyes were the darker blue of the sky away from the sunset, with streaks of light blue.

"Still asleep. Headache."

"*C'yo,*" Wennië cussed. "I'll go get him up."

"Sit and I'll get the toast." My mom offered as Wennië went up-stairs. "Are you ready for the prank?"

I'd forgotten. "Sure." I plopped down in my normal seat. I'd wait until Nol and Wennië were out to go get the crystal.

"Here." She set the pieces that Wennië had started in front of me.

"Matina helped." I took my first bite while my mother poured me some breakfast tea.

She paused with my cup half full and raised her amethyst eyes to look at me. "You went into Metina's?"

"With An'di before she left." We ate in silence for a while, listening to Wennië's soft tenor from upstairs. She'd make Nol drink more of her medicinal tea. It worked, but the stuff was horrid. She claimed that medicine was supposed to taste bad, otherwise we'd drink it all the time.

After I'd had my toast and my tea was almost gone, I was awake enough to explain more. "I proved that I'm perfectly fine in her shop. But, I see why you don't want me in there. All I wanted to do was rearrange everything to give it some sort of order."

"And that's coming from my impulsive, energetic daughter."

"I like to organize pretty things." I thought of my dresser and all the cute trinkets on it. "We can't let Nol in there."

My mom laughed into her tea.

"Don't let me in where?" Nol grumbled from the top of the stairs.

"Metina's shop. We love you, dear, but you're bound to break something." My mom explained as I finished my tea.

"I was afraid if I breathed wrong, the shelves would collapse."

"Gee, such faith you hold in me." Nol's lips twisted as he pouted.

"Grab some food, grumpy. We have to go."

Nol grunted and snatched a muffin off the counter. "Bye."

"No hugs?" Wennië sat at the table once more.

Nol and I turned at the door. "No, you made me get up."

I kept some distance between the grumpy boy. "How's your head?" I asked as we left my house.

"Murë made me drink tea. I can still taste it. So gross."

"Good morning, you two." Gil came up and gave me a kiss on the head. He didn't pull me to him, but he winked his black eye. "How's your injuries?" He had bandages on his knuckles and temple, and bruises up his arms.

Nol grunted, then tipped his chin to Gil.

"Same," Gil said, answering the male nonverbal language as we began walking again.

"My murë gave me willow bark last night," Gil said. "The inflammation is gone, but I'm stiff. Wennië's stuff works, but I'll pass any day. When are you talking to the headmaster?"

"Laro has morning classes, so not until the end of the day. Murë said he went in early to tell the headmaster what happened."

"They need to be stopped. Unfortunately for us, our beating will be the tipping point."

"You can't be sure of that," I said.

We didn't talk the rest of the way, too tired—or in their case sore—to think of conversation topics.

"This is where I must leave you, my friends."

Nol didn't respond with words, and Gil only gave me another kiss on the head.

"I don't have the capacity to listen to lectures today," Nol admitted after Gil left. "Murë said I have to—not let them think they won."

"You'll need to pretend. I'll help you later." I patted him on the arm.

"For this class, civics and magical applications. I'm screwed for the others."

"Tell them you're not feeling well."

"Won't work—never does."

"Maybe—"

"Hallë, enough. I can't think, and nothing you suggest has any merit. Stop trying to make me feel better."

I clenched my jaw and counted to ten. "So sorry for trying." I left him in the hall and walked to my assistant desk for foreign language. He wasn't getting any help now.

DURING MY FREE PERIOD, I ran home for the crystal that I'd forgotten on the dresser. Lahiem and Carena planned to come in after lessons today to work on their potions. Unless I waited a week…I'd see how things went.

"Nevie?" my mother called from somewhere in the house.

"I forgot the crystal!" With no other explanation, I ran up and grabbed it; it was glowing bright blue in the sun. What if the sunlight interacted with the moonlight charge?

"Nevie, wait," she called again before I ran out, her voice high and worried.

"Yeah?"

"Your prank? I'm proud of you. Show them what you can do."

Too stunned and emotional to speak, I ran and gave her a hug. Two in less than twenty-four hours.

But maybe… "The crystal had to charge in the moonlight, but I left it in the sun all morning. Do you think that might be a problem? Should I wait?"

"It shouldn't have any effect on it."

"Great, I have to go get this done then. Um…thanks, Murë."

Without another thought, I ran back to the school. I took the front steps two at time and hurried down to Professor Jerric's classroom, keeping my eyes open for any sign of Lahiem and Carena. I grabbed the bottles from the back and hid in the smallest lab.

Instead of dumping the liquid onto the crystals, I decided to slowly drip it on top. It dried instantly, nothing else. I couldn't even see a reaction. Boring. I poured the measured oil over them.

Now the *Mellorian* invoking phrase. "*Daetern*," I whispered. The crystals glowed for a moment and then settled back to normal. I wrapped two back up in the paper. Class would start in five minutes, so I dropped my tester crystal in the water and waited. The water around the crystal started bubbling right away. A few heartbeats later it shrank, slowly at first, then it picked up speed. The water began to turn blue and heat up. I hadn't expected that. The last granule dissolved, and the water started boiling violently. The whole bowl of water was gone with two minutes to spare to get to Professor Asin's class. Not much of a show—for me. Watching it happen to what I thought was my potion would scare me senseless. I'd make sure to jump out right after, before they panicked too much.

The rest of the day went so slow.

"What is going on with your day, my love?" Gil came up beside me while I wasn't paying attention.

I blew air through my pursed lips. "I have a secret."

Gil's eyebrows shot up.

"I found a prank, but I don't want Nol to know. He doesn't think I can do this spell." I swallowed as I said it out loud. My *muranildo* doubted my abilities. He was on Asin's side. "I told my murë and Metina. It's advanced, but...He'll see, they'll see."

"Is this about Asin yesterday."

My throat got tight as I tried not to cry. He kissed my cheek. "I'm sorry he did that to you. It wasn't right."

"He acted like he was doing me a favor."

Gil closed his eyes and pulled me in. "Can I walk you to class?"

"You'll be late to yours." I kissed his cheek. "And you have Rassel. He's a jerk, plus he might use you to get back at me. He hasn't been very pleasant since he got in trouble."

He began pulling me through the hall anyway. Honestly, it wasn't much farther. "Ah, true. I haven't heard any of the students complain, though. I think most of them are on your side."

"That's a rarity."

He nuzzled my cheek. "I'm always on your side."

I rolled my eyes. "That's expected. You are my boyfriend."

Nol found us as we were almost at the door to my class. "What's wrong?"

I tried to pull away from Gil, but he wouldn't open his arms. "Nothing."

"Did Asin say something again? We can hide another *quette* dragon in his desk. Better yet—"

"It isn't—" Yes, it was Asin, actually. "We already did the *quette* dragon."

"We'll think of something worse. Are you going to civics?" He looked down the hall. "I'm in, if you want to skip. Gil hates math, I hate civics."

"I like civics. Gil, you have to get going before you're late." I pushed him toward the other end of the hall. I stepped back and started pushing Nol into class. Nol tripped, and I fell right on top of him. "Sorry!"

Gil came and helped us both up, kissed me on the cheek, and hurried off to class.

"Nol, are you hurt?"

"No." But he was favoring his left arm and his face was bright red. "Let's go, if you insist on going."

"Nevie! Nolan! Get in here. By the Stars, Nolan, you need to be more careful," Professor Baslen hollered from her door, her old, wavering voice straining. "I swear you're more clumsy than my uncle was at twelve hundred. Come, come." She ushered us in.

11

Nol slid his book and notes into his bag as we gathered our classwork after class. "Are you going to wait for us?"

Had I forgotten something? "Wait for you?"

"The meeting. Will you be there afterward?"

Urro, that would be the supportive thing to do. "Uh..." I thought about the timing. By the end of their meeting, Lahiem and Carena should have shown up, and my prank would last all of two minutes. "Sure."

"If it's too much, don't do it." He sneered, adjusting his shoulder straps so they weren't trapping his hair, and then left without saying goodbye. Ugh, he was so grumpy today!

I waited until Nol turned the corner before I bolted the other way, thinking about all that I still needed to do. *Oh, please let there be enough time.*

I sped into the room and hid my bag in the back. I filled two potion bowls with plain water first. Next, I secured lids to Carena's and Lahiem's potions and carefully brought them into the back room, one by one. Making sure their potions were safe was more important than getting caught. I unwrapped the crystals and set one next to each bowl of water.

Now the waiting. I stood right inside the entrance to listen for any sounds of movement. Forever later—or more like five minutes—Carena's high laugh echoed down the hall. This was it! It wouldn't take me but a few seconds to hide, so I listened to their chatter until they were almost there, then dropped in the crystals. The crystals started steaming just like the tester, but I couldn't stay and watch. Lahiem and Carena were around the corner! I scooted around the back just as the *endai* were walking in.

Carena noticed first.

"*C'yo*, Lahiem! What's happening? They're burning." Was she crying?

"No, they're boiling. We have to save them." Lahiem hissed. "Ow, it splashed me."

Maybe I should have rethought this.

"Don't touch it!" Lahiem yelled as Carena hissed. I peeked around the door to see Carena run to the faucet and rinse her hand.

"Don't use water, Carena." Lahiem came over with a towel, patting the liquid off.

"Can we stop it?"

"There's nothing to stop," Lahiem said. "They're gone."

I jumped out as soon as I heard Lahiem, flipping my arms out wide. "Surprise! Your potions are safe!"

Carena and Lahiem stared, tears streaking Carena's face while Lahiem held the towel to her hand.

"I didn't think you'd touch it, though. Sorry about that."

"You—how?" Carena sputtered, looking from Lahiem to me.

"They're here in the back, Carena. I would never ruin your potions."

Lahiem started laughing first, looking down at the bowls, then up at me. "Where did you find this one at? Nevie, this was great."

"Great? I ought to choke you." Carena shook her fist, but her lips were curved up in a grin. "You had me so scared."

"How did you do it?" Lahiem asked.

"Infused a crystal to time the reaction of evaporation."

"This was a traditional spell?"

"Yes. I found it in the library. Nol didn't think I could do it, but I did! I did it just like you told me, Lahiem!"

"You sure did, Nevie. Good job," Carena said. Her smile faltered and she started scratching her hand. "But this stuff is still burning."

"Do you have the book? Is there a neutralizing spell or component?" Lahiem asked.

"Just a moment." I dodged back and grabbed my bag. Carena called out in pain just as I came back in. Her hands covered her face, and she continued to cry. "What's wrong?" This couldn't be from my spell. I tested it out and it went fine. Unless she was allergic to the ingredients? Oh, no! I never thought of that.

Lahiem cried out, startling me. They couldn't both be allergic to an ingredient.

"Nevie, get the book. Quick, it's still reacting."

I dropped the bag on the table and yanked the book out, flipping through the pages.

"Lahiem, I don't understand. I tested it out and this didn't happen to me." My hands shook as I found the right page and set it in front of Lahiem.

Lahiem was sweating, and her arm was yellow and red with white boils. "We," she panted, "touched the vapor and liquid. *C'yo*, this hurts. Let me look." Lahiem placed a finger over the spell and scanned the words. "Here it is. Get salt. Hurry."

I threw open the cupboard with the dry supplies. There wasn't much salt in here. *Please, Mother, let there be enough.* Carena hadn't stopped crying.

"Lahiem!" I ran over, showing her the salt. "There isn't much. I have to go get more."

"Pour it on her face."

"Carena, move your hands!" I had to set the salt container down to pull her hands away. Her entire face was covered in white and pink boils, and her eyes were almost swollen shut. She tried to bring her hands up again. "I have to—"

She stopped screaming as she passed out on the floor. With a shaky hand I poured the salt over her face slow enough that it collected on her forehead and upper lip instead of spilling off. I set the empty container next to me as I patted at the salt.

"Lahiem, it's working!" Sure enough, as I pushed some salt around on her face with my thumb, the skin underneath was less red. "It's going down quickly. I'll run and get more salt."

Lahiem fell to the floor.

"Nevie, go get Jerric, too."

"All right, but Lahiem, it's working." It would take more time to get him, and she needed the salt now.

"Go, please." By her pained look I didn't argue. She knew something else.

The test worked for me! I hadn't—what had I done? "Lahiem?"

"Nevie, look at me. Look at me! This isn't your fault. No matter what, this isn't your fault. Go! Hurry."

I nodded, too in the moment to think much beyond getting them help. How Lahiem figured it wasn't my fault was a mystery. Jerric's room was two doors down. I flung open his door, but he wasn't there. I kept running; sometimes they had meetings after lessons. I ran around the corner and almost collided with Jerric.

He had his bag on his shoulder. I'd just caught him. "What's wrong, Nevie?"

"Lahiem, Carena. I messed up. Help."

He sprinted along with me back to the lab. "What happened?"

The explanation was too long to explain while we ran.

"My prank."

"Which lab?"

"Second. I have to get salt." I halted at lab one while Jerric ran ahead into lab two. This one had a full container of salt. Maybe this would turn out fine. As I returned to the lab, salt clutched to my chest, I thought I heard Nol call my name. But that didn't matter now.

Jerric held Lahiem in his arms, gripping her hand as they talked in hushed tones.

"I got more salt. Lahiem, hang on." Falling beside her, I poured some onto her red hand.

"We touched the vapors," Lahiem said, panting. "It's not Nevie's fault. It was an accident. Tell them—"

Jerric was nodding. I went back to Carena, still unconscious, and poured salt on her hands and patted more onto her face.

"Nevie, stop." Professor Jerric grabbed my arm and took the empty container out of my hand. "It's no use. They're gone."

"They can't be." My voice faltered. "The salt—it's going to—Lahiem said to get the salt. She said it'll neutralize it." I broke at the end, unsure if Jerric even understood me. "It's working on Carena."

"What happened?"

Jerric and I looked up, finding Nol standing in the entrance. I looked back at our professor. He licked his lips, looked at me, then back at Nol.

"There was a chemical accident. Nolan, go get, uh—Professor Mejorë." Jerric shook my arm to get my attention. "Nevie, it's okay. This was an accident. Lahiem told me."

"A chemical accident? How?"

I stared at Carena's open—but unseeing—eyes. Her face was one huge burn. My eyes dropped to my hands in my lap. Nol knelt beside me. His hand came into my line of sight, and he placed his fingers on Carena's neck, his breaths quick and shallow. He already knew, that's why he hadn't left. "They're dead. What happened? Hallë, look at me."

I wasn't brave enough to face him. He'd been right.

"Nolan, I need you to go. Let me"—Jerric glanced at me, then back at Nol—"get the chemical."

Nol crawled over to Lahiem and checked for her pulse. "What chemical was this?" He crawled back to me, his voice shaking. Nol sat back on his heels and wiped his face with his arm. "Did you do this, Hallë?"

My lips trembled. I lost it and fell over Carena.

"Please, give me some time to sort this out," Jeric said. "They'll blame Nevie for this. You know they will."

"Was it her fault?" Nol paused. "You did that spell, didn't you? The one I told you not to use for the prank."

Jerric didn't ask again. I didn't speak.

"I told you it was too advanced for you."

I looked up. His face was red from tears and anger.

"I did everything right. I checked with Metina. I tested it and it didn't do this for me. They touched it and it just started… We were all laughing. It worked and then—"

"I told you the author's work was immoral and your control with traditional spells isn't good enough. You murdered our friends."

"No. It wasn't supposed to go—"

"But it did and you murdered them." Nol shoved me.

"That's enough, Nolan. You don't know what you're saying. It was an accident. Lahiem told me before—"

"Before she died? Of course, she would say that! She always catered to her. You can't use traditional spells, Hallë."

I started. Nol had never yelled at me like this, nor had he mentioned Lahiem doing anything like that. "But it—"

"I don't even know you anymore." Nol stood up. "I revoke our *Muranilde* bond. You are dead to me. Dead, Hallanevaë."

"Nol—"

"You will never call me that again," he said, his voice breaking. Nol—Twynolan backed up, wiped at his tears, and left us.

"Nevie, listen. Calm down, breathe, and listen. You never confirmed which spell you used. Do not say anything to anyone. It isn't your fault."

"But it is. I found the spell."

"Just because you cast the spell doesn't mean your intent was to harm anyone. Any spell can go wrong. It was an accident."

"They're dead. They're dead and it's because of me. Nol—Twynolan—he's gone—"

"Enough of that." Jerric grabbed my shoulders. "I will get your parents. I'll talk to Nolan. We'll sort this out."

I nodded because I didn't need to say anything. The proof was in my notes, in the book itself. Metina knew and my mother.

"There she is." Nol—Twynolan didn't sound much like himself as he pointed at me. Asin and Rassel were standing around him.

"Nevie?" Asin asked in a low voice.

"I knew the freak was dangerous." Rassel spat out his words. "Just like her grandmother. She can't be trusted."

Asin came through the door first and grabbed my arm.

"Stop. This isn't her fault."

"Jerric, stop defending her. She's not getting out of this one," Asin said.

Rassel walked to my other side and took my other arm, yanking me away from Jerric and almost tearing my arm out of the socket. Together, they dragged me across the room and out the door. I tried to get up, but their longer strides made me stumble and fall again.

"Nevie! Don't say a word to them. You know the system better than any student. Ask for Cyaisn."

"Get up." Rassel shook me so hard that I bit my tongue. "Get up, you freak." He yanked me up until I was standing. Again, they started walking, but I couldn't match their steps.

"She..." Nol's words faltered. "She can't walk between you two like that, you idiots. Her legs aren't that long."

The two *endao* didn't respond to Twynolan's words, just continued to drag me down the hall. Other professors who were still in the building stopped and stared with looks of confusion and curiosity. Asin and Rassel dragged me out of the Hall of Knowledge, across the spiral, and to the Hall of Justice. Once there, the officer on duty, Brendelin, met us in front.

"She killed two students with magic. Arrest her," Rassel demanded.

Brendelin's brows furrowed. "Where? I can't just take her in without evidence."

"Tell him." Rassel shook me.

"Hey! Let go of her. I'm not arresting her until I find out what's going on. Nevie, go back and sit in my office. You have to stay here, though. Do you hear me?"

Asin and Rassel still hadn't let me go.

Brendelin held me under my arms. "Let her go. Now, or I'll arrest you for assaulting her. *C'yo.* Come on, I'll take you back."

"You need to lock her up."

"I know how to do my job," he snapped before he led me into the Justice building and away from them. "You wait for me right here." Brendelin guided me to a chair in a small, quiet room off the main entrance. "Nevie? Can you tell me what happened?"

I said nothing as my teeth chattered.

He touched my arm where Rassel had gripped it and I jerked. Brendelin frowned and ground his teeth. "Will you stay here while I find out what I can?" He pulled some hair off my face. "Nevie, can you acknowledge what I said? Can you stay here?"

Teeth chattering, body shaking, I tried to meet his eyes and nod, but I started crying as soon as I saw his pale hazel eyes.

12

Brendelin came back, and without saying anything, he took my hand and guided me to the detention cells. Hollow and knowing my fate, I said nothing, did nothing, as he locked me in the cell. I stood in the middle of the tiny thing and waited until Brendelin left. I dropped to the floor and didn't move. What was the point? I'd killed my friends. Nothing else mattered.

I cried whenever my mind wandered back to what happened. My thoughts went right to Twynolan's words after that. I was dead to him; we were no longer *muranildi*. I hoped, for his sake, it worked. If we were still connected, he'd die soon after they executed me, because that's what they did to people when they used magic to kill people. An automatic death sentence. I prayed to the Mother to spare him.

There were no windows, just solid stone walls in a round room with a low ceiling. Twynolan could press his palms to it. The only light came from windows down near the front doors. They provided a bed with two blankets, a table, and a solid waste receptacle hidden by a privacy curtain. The wooden door had slats in it, so if I felt so inclined, I could look out and see the bare stone wall of the opposite cell through those door slats. Not that I got up much. I had to relieve myself once, then went back to the floor. My growling stomach woke me from a fitful sleep.

"Nevie?" Brendelin called my name, but I didn't respond. "Sit up, I've got your dinner. You've got to stay strong in here. I saw the lab. It looks bad, but Jerric is defending you." He didn't need to be so nice to me. I sat up as he opened the door and walked in. "The *Aore* Junae and *Loret*

Maeson said you can't have any visitors for now." He set a tray on the table and crouched down to my level. My stomach growled at the smell of the herbs and vegetables in the soup. "All the facts need to be sorted out before a decision can be made. Can you tell me anything about what happened?"

Brendelin was being kind so he could get me to talk. Perhaps my family couldn't come to me, but I was allowed a legal counselor. Brendelin knew I knew the system, so I didn't understand why he was even asking.

"All right, go ahead and eat. Maybe you'll give me some information tomorrow."

I cleared my throat. "Cyaisn."

"What?" His shoulders dropped, knowing exactly what I'd said.

"Cyaisn. I'll only speak to her." She was one of the three legal counselors in the city and Jerric's wife.

He sighed, heavily. "This won't help you."

"I know my rights. I want Cyaisn."

"I'll see if she will come."

Why wouldn't she? It was her duty to help residents of *Rudairn*. Even murderers.

"Nevie?" Someone was whispering. "Nevie, wake up."

At first, I couldn't remember why I was lying on the floor. Was Nol whispering, or was that Laro or Murë? They whispered again. My eyes opened and everything came back to me. I squeezed my eyes shut as tears welled up.

"Who's there?" I whispered back, because no one but Brendelin was allowed to be in here.

"It's Gileal. Oh, Nevie. Come to me, love."

I stayed where I was on the floor. "How are you back here?"

"I snuck in. Laro has a way in for when prisoners ask for clergy. You can do that, if you want. Laro says all you need to do is ask. The council can't deny you a clergy visit."

"No."

"Everything is crazy. Your parents are scared. They've denied your father a traveling *meril* to get your grandmother. Jerric is defending you at all costs. Nolan is freaking out. He wants to apologize, but they won't let him in here."

"No, Gil. He revoked our bond. I'm dead to him."

"He didn't mean those words, Nevie. You know how he is when he gets angry. He always says the worst things. You need to hold on. I'll tell you everything that happens. I'll be here whenever I'm able. Nevie, come to the door and take my hand."

I shook my head and lay back down. "You don't need to come. There's nothing anyone can do. They're gone. They're gone, Gil." Admitting it to Gil brought on more crying, and I couldn't stop. I don't know if he stayed, I don't know when I fell asleep. It didn't matter. Nothing mattered anymore.

THE CREAK OF THE entrance door and Brendelin's steps reverberated down the hall and through my cell. His boots came into my line of sight on the floor as he stopped at my door.

My cell door opened and Brendelin picked up my dinner from last night and replaced it with breakfast. I still wasn't going to eat it. "Nevie, you need to eat and drink something." He sighed. "I'll be back in fifteen minutes to escort you to the shower. Your murë brought some clothes. I, uh—sent in your request for Cyaisn. Please eat, Nevie." Then he was gone.

I didn't need to eat. Nothing could be done until my grandmother was back, but I doubted she could do anything. The law was clear. Kill with magic, forfeit your life.

Brendelin, true to his word, came back later—whether that was fifteen minutes or not didn't matter, as I was stuck here and time didn't matter. I knew the law, I knew my fate now. The one I ruined. Shattered. I was supposed to make things better! I was supposed to change the *Amura*

Ore for the better. This wasn't better, not planned or what I wanted. I couldn't advocate for our people in the capital when I murdered my own friends. And now Brendelin wanted me to take a shower?

"Nevie, stop feeling sorry for yourself and take a shower."

Sorry for myself? That wasn't what this was.

"I want to talk to Cyaisn."

"Get up so you don't smell bad for her when she gets to come."

That held merit. I pulled myself off the floor. Brendelin tried helping, but he took my arm where Rassel had held me. He quickly released me when I cried out. Yes, it hurt. No, I wasn't overreacting. They hated me.

Brendelin made me walk in front of him to the showers at the end of the hall. He opened the shower room door. It was a long room, with drains in each corner under a showering area. When he opened the faucet, water poured out from the ceiling along the line from drain to drain. This was such a waste of time! A waste of resources. I turned off the shower and lowered myself to the floor against the wall. The water collected, swirling in a puddle around the drain until most of it was gone. Just like my life, down the drain.

"Nevie? The towel is on the hook for you. I left your clothes on the chair."

My cheek touched the cold stone as I watched that bit of defiant water refusing to go down the drain. *Rudairn* had three law officers and one of them was female. I didn't know their schedules, but I doubted Brendelin would risk coming in here himself. He asked if I was done three more times before he threatened to come in.

"Cyaisn!" I yelled.

Ajurelle, the female guard, came in some time later. She wasn't amused. "Get up and take a shower, Nevie."

"Cyaisn."

"The only thing you need Cyaisn for is legal counsel. Take a shower before I make you take one."

Like she could. I rolled over and looked at the wall. Ajurelle grabbed me under my armpits.

"No!" I struggled against her until she let me go. I got up on my knees and crawled back to my spot. Freezing water cascaded from above. "Stop! Turn it off," I screamed.

"Not until you're clean. You can sit there and throw a tantrum. I'll keep dragging you back under, or you can strip and clean yourself."

I sucked in air, coughed when I inhaled water, and screamed at her, coughing and sputtering at the end.

"Hate me all you want. You're angry, fine. But get your ass up and take care of yourself for that speck of hope that everyone will get you out of here."

"It doesn't matter!"

"Why?"

I inhaled, ready to scream at her just why I deserved this, but thought better of it. "Cyaisn! I am entitled to representation."

She went to yell back, inches from my face, but pursed her lips and stood up. I was right and she had no argument. "Get undressed and clean yourself, before I do. And I'm not going to be gentle."

Seeing the truth in her eyes, I backed up and undressed. This was so pointless. I grit my teeth and peeled the soaking shirt off my arms, then fought my wet pants. She handed me the soap and left the room. "You have five minutes, and then I will make sure you're clean. Do you understand me?"

I glared, holding the soap, wanting to throw it at her.

"Do you understand me?"

What else could I do? Fighting would only get me in more trouble.

"Yes." I turned away from her and started scrubbing. I hated her. I hated them. I hated everything.

"EVERYONE IS WORKING TO get you out," Gil told me by the glow of his light globe. "Your mother and Nolan's parents are helping Jerric find proof that it wasn't your magic that caused it. If they can prove that, then the council can't sentence you. Where is the book you used?"

Now that was interesting. I sat up and scooted to the door. "I left it in the lab, next to—next to Lahiem. Gil, I did everything right. My magic must be what caused it. Twynolan is right, my magic is out of control."

Gil reached through the bars and clasped my hand. "Nolan didn't mean that. He was just upset. You know how he gets."

I had to get my voice under control before I could say the rest. "He revoked our bond. I'm dead to him. You can't take that back, Gil."

"Nevie—"

"He won't help."

"He is helping. Right now, Nolan is trying to find a traveling *meril* discreetly with your father."

"What do you mean?"

"We're trying to get word to your grandmother, but *Loret* Maeson and *Aore* Junae denied your father's and Wennië's requests for a traveling *meril*. Nevie, it can't be a coincidence that this happened when Zella is out of town. They set you up."

"No, they didn't. I found the book, I chose the spell, it was all me." Gil went to argue, but I changed the subject. "What about Cyaisn? Why hasn't she—or any of them—come to see me? I need legal counsel." My friends had been dead for over twenty-four hours. No one had come to represent me.

"The council members say you're too dangerous for visitors. They're talking about a proxy and sentencing you without Zella. What does that entail?"

"They'll contact the district delegation or perhaps the capital *Amura Ore* to request a third member to be present for an emergency decision. What I did was wrong, but this can wait until Yalu returns. I'm not going anywhere or hurting anyone. Unless—" I paused as I sorted everything out. "—they claim bias. With another member, it might work in my favor."

"How so?"

"This new person doesn't know me. Everyone knows the animosity toward my family, but they don't know me. The proxy should look at the facts instead of emotions. This is good, Gil."

"They're barring you from legal counsel, Nevie. That isn't right."

"Let's just hope the proxy that is chosen will have compassion."

"I'm skeptical. The *Amura Ore* has gotten away with so many transgressions." I could hear Gil's teeth grinding.

"They have, but you can't stop them."

"We'll make it better," Gil vowed. I didn't have the heart to remind him I wouldn't be fighting that fight anymore.

13

"It's time, Nevie." Brendelin came in between breakfast and lunch the next day. Impressive. They got everything together in less than two days. "Gileal is going to walk with us."

"I'm not supposed to see anyone but the guards."

"Yeah, well, he's not supposed to sneak in here at night either."

Of course, Brendelin knew.

"You still have a bit of time. Nolan found a *meril*."

My stomach flipped. "Why would he help? He's the one who brought Rassel and Asin to me."

Brendelin didn't say anything for a while. "Sometimes people say things they don't mean when they're angry. Your *muranildo*—"

"He broke our bond."

"Do you really think you can break something like that?"

"I hope so, because he'll die soon after I do if it can't be broken."

I got up when I heard the quiet creak of the door. I held my hands out for him to bind them, but instead he guided me out the door and left me standing there to shut it.

"Aren't you going to put the wrist cuffs on?"

"You don't need them." He pulled the front door open, turned, and waited. "Come on."

"But you'll get in trouble."

"It was an accident. Everyone knows it, whether they'll admit it or not. It shouldn't be like this. You're a kid, and I'll be damned to the Starless Abyss before I bind your hands."

My throat tightened and my tears fell as we walked out of the Hall of Justice, where my trial should have been held. "Why—" I stretched my neck and coughed as I tried to talk again. "Why isn't my trial here."

"I don't know."

"But—"

"Nevie." Gil jumped next to me on the other side of Brendelin. "Nolan has a *meril* and he's getting Zella and An'di now. We'll delay as long as we can."

Why would he turn me in and then help them save me? "Gil—"

"I promise he will bring your grandmother. Your parents are already in the hall."

At the base of our city's Tree of Connection, two groups of people had gathered near the entrance, watching our progression. A range of emotions—stunned to curious, anger to hatred—watched us. Jemi and Enyco stood close to the front of the smaller group, then I spotted other students and all their parents. Dozens of people watched me.

"How could you!" Lorie screamed. She hadn't even liked Lahiem and Carena.

"You're a freak, you're a freak family. You deserve to die," Tessa, an adult I didn't know well, screamed. Someone else echoed her sentiment and others found their own.

"How can you defend that murderer, Gileal?"

"The Mother cursed Nolan when She made you his *muranildë*."

I cringed at that one.

"Ignore them, Nevie. Hold your head high," Gil murmured close to me. But I watched my feet instead of meeting their angry, hateful eyes.

On the other side, we passed those that just wanted to watch or didn't know what to think.

"Nevie?" Another student, Cerrel, yelled above the others. "It was an accident, right? We know you wouldn't really hurt Lahiem and Carena."

"This isn't the end, Nevie," said another girl. I kept my eyes down, unable to meet the eyes of those who knew my friends. Some voices I recognized, some I didn't, but they stayed outside as we descended under the ancient tree.

Pearl white iridescent tiles covered the hall down into the underside of the tree—the same kind that were in the capital's Tree of Connection. Magic light orbs gave off a soft glow that reflected off the tiles. Once out of the hall and under the enormous tree, Brendelin took us to the first of the two sentencing rooms.

Brendelin knocked on a door made of gnarled dark wood with a swirling design of narrow pearl tiles. Ajurelle opened the door from the other side and moved out of the way. In the front of the room, the two city council members sat in their seats: *Loret* Maeson, the only junior member, and *Aore* Junae, the other senior member besides Yalu. My grandmother's seat was filled by Rassel—not another assembly member. Fear sliced through me. Rassel couldn't be a proxy!

My parents were in the front, faces puffy and red. Twynolan's parents stood next to them; Wennië had her arm around my mother. My father and Edvic watched as we made our way to the front. Gil's parents stood on the other side of Edvic, their worried looks watching us. I lowered my eyes to the floor, scared but resigned to my fate. With Rassel here, I was doomed.

"Brendelin, why isn't Hallanevaë bound?"

"She won't cause any harm," Brendelin answered Rassel.

"Her actions two days ago prove that she's dangerous. I saw what she did with my own eyes."

How were they getting away with this?

"She's not going to be bound for this." Brendelin stood firm, allowing no argument. He was my jailer, after all.

"It was an accident!" I hadn't noticed Jerric in here until he shouted. "I heard testimony from Lahiem before she died. It wasn't Nevie's fault. Rassel saw nothing."

"Silence."

"Honored council members." My head came up. Cyaisn stood beside her husband. "Nevie deserves a fair trial."

"Cyaisn, we've already heard your argument for the defendant," *Aore* Junae announced.

Argument? She hadn't even talked to me. "Council members, I have not been given any legal counsel. By *Amura Ore* law, seven hundred—"

"Hallanevaë, you will only speak when we give you permission," *Loret* Maeson snapped.

"That's not legal!" I yelled. Yes, I was guilty, but I still knew my rights.

"Your actions have deemed you a terrorist and as such, your rights are forfeit," *Aore* Junae claimed—illegally.

Cyaisn gasped. "What?"

"That's not—"

"That's exactly what it is, Hallanevaë. You are a threat to society that can't be controlled," *Aore* Junae said, interrupting me again.

"Council members, please?" my mother pleaded. "That wasn't her intention."

"Which is even more disturbing. If your daughter can do this without intention, what will she do when she decides to lash out? We can't have that."

"I demand you wait for *Aore* Zella to be here!" Cyaisn yelled. "There must be two senior members, *Aore* Junae. Zella has a right to defend her granddaughter."

"Her argument would be biased. This is why we requested senior council members from the capital to make up for her absence," *Aore* Junae said. "However, they chose to stay and trust our judgement in this matter. They've heard the situation and will support our decision."

"You don't know the situation. You haven't let anyone talk to Nevie!" Cyaisn said. "I demand to see the capital council's decision in writing. I move for this trial to be postponed until I can confirm that decision."

"Denied. We received Jerric's account," *Aore* Junae said. "Lahiem and Carena were found on the floor, dead, with Hallanevaë's notes open next to them. Her detailed accounts of her work are all the confession we need. The spell she invented was meticulously planned out and thought through."

"Invented?" I whispered to Gil. "I didn't invent it, I followed the directions for the spell in the book."

"We can't find the book. I told you last night, didn't you hear me?"

"But it was—"

"I thought we might be searching in the wrong place. No one has found it," Gil explained.

"Council members," I cried out, voice raised. "I did not invent this spell. It was a traditional spell I found in the library."

"So you claim, but where is this book? Tell us where you left it, and we will consider it."

I looked back at Cyaisn and Jerric. He was the only one who had had a chance to see it. Right? He'd seen it? But Jerric shook his head at me. Then where was it? "I left it next to Lahiem. She read the spell and found that salt neutralizes it. She had it in her hands."

"It wasn't there."

Not the best choice. "Maybe you shouldn't rush this and actually do some investigating then," I snarled.

"You will not tell us what we should and should not do in our investigation."

"What investigation? Your proxy is one of the teachers who hates me and will do anything to get rid of me."

"That is not true, Nevie. I do not hate you. Sometimes I am unhappy with the choices you make. And admittedly, I have gotten frustrated with your disability in the past—"

"It's not a disability," I shouted.

"We try to be patient and offer you alternative work to help you."

"My daughter's magic isn't a disability, Rassel, and you know it," my dad's voice bellowed around the room, not at all like his normal calm demeanor.

"Enough." *Aore* Junae called everything to order with that one word. "Hallanevaë, come to the front, child." Shaking, I walked away from Brendelin. "Gileal, you cannot come with her."

Gil pulled me close, careful of my arm. His lips trembled as he kissed my temple, kissed my forehead, and wrapped his arms around me.

"They'll be here any second. Take your time walking up. Please, believe me. Nolan is coming."

I turned and tipped my chin to meet his eyes. "Gil," I whispered. "He's not coming. I'm dead to him."

"No."

"I'm dead to him. Please take care of him. I pray the bond did break so that he may live a full life without me. He doesn't deserve to die because of my horrible actions."

"Nevie!" Raj's high voice pierced the room. The door thumped closed as she ran to the front.

"Rajamë, stop," *Aore* Junae called. She didn't listen as she skidded to a halt beside Brendelin.

"Gileal, they're coming. Stall."

"Ajurelle, do not let anyone else through that door," Rassel yelled.

"That is not your order to make, Rassel," *Aore* Junae said.

"Let us see our daughter. Move, Brendelin." My parents came up to stand behind Raj and Brendelin. Was he trying to help stall this?

"Brendelin, if you can't control this situation, you will be stripped of your title," *Loret* Maeson said. "Keep them away. Gileal, you will back up now."

I pulled out of Gil's arms. Brendelin's extended arm prevented me from seeing everyone behind us. This also kept Gil from leaving my side.

Brendelin stumbled as my parents pushed on him, but he stayed at his post. "Nevie, I'm sorry. I can't let them come through."

"Hallanevaë, come forward now."

I heard my mom crying from behind Brendelin. I shuffled closer to the council members, and when I looked back, I noticed they'd stopped pushing on Brendelin. Over his shoulder, my dad's scared, worried eyes locked with mine. There was nothing left to stall.

Brendelin only made Gil step back after I got in the sentencing circle. When Gil tried to move toward me, Brendelin placed his hand on his chest. "Don't give them an excuse to throw you out."

"Hallanevaë, turn and face us," *Aore* Junae said.

Shaking and barely able to focus on any one thing, I obeyed.

"You have been convicted of murdering Lahiem and Carena using of your own design. Your own notes of the design and methods are our proof." The room went silent at his words. No trial, nothing. "The law calls for your death. There are no stipulations to this."

My mom wailed and I spun around. She dropped to the floor, my dad crouched over her, his shoulders heaving. Wennië couldn't take her eyes off me as Edvic stood at her back, holding her shoulders.

"However!" At *Aore* Junae's loud word, my mom's sobs stopped. "However," he continued in a normal voice, "we have a unique predicament. Your *muranildo* would die if we carry out your punishment. Nolan has done nothing wrong, and we cannot ethically allow him to die for your actions."

Everyone held their breath as *Aore* Junae looked around the room. "We have decided your punishment is exile. You are hereby deemed a *savilë*. Your name will never be heard throughout *Aemina* after we leave this room. You are no longer *Aeminan*."

Exiled? Had anyone ever been exiled before? I knew of the *Savile* title, but none of my studies mentioned a specific person in history sentenced to exile.

"Are you listening to your sentence, Hallanevaë?"

At my name, I pulled my eyes away from the two sets of parents who'd raised Twynolan and me and looked at the three corrupt *endai* in front of me. This was unprecedented. No one was given their sentencing the same day as the trial. But then—this wasn't a trial. I was guilty, but I knew this was wrong. Everyone knew this was wrong. There shouldn't be such a swift sentencing. It had only been two days since the incident. Normally it would take them no sooner than a month!

"Hallanevaë?" *Aore* Junae spoke, much softer than before.

"Yes—yes, I hear you." I shifted from foot to foot and tried to calm my racing heart.

"Banishment has not happened in over two thousand years, but it was successful when it was done. We are sending you to the *Rosava* realm. Their magic is different there, and you will be of no threat to them and their ways. We feel this is the best choice for everyone, especially since you are still a child. You will be safe there. Do you understand this sentencing?"

"Another realm is excessive!" Cyaisn yelled.

"Cyaisn, if you can't control yourself, you will be removed from the room," *Loret* Maeson snapped.

"Hallanevaë, do you understand?" *Aore* Junae asked.

I nodded, hands over my face, heart aching. I would live with the shame of killing my friends for however long I lived.

"Nevie?" Rassel said. Surprised at his gentler tone, I looked up. "You need to pay attention."

I sniffled and nodded.

"The only reason we are sparing your life is because of Nolan." *Aore* Junae lifted his eyes and looked at the door as someone on the other side started slamming it with something. "You are now only living for your *muranildo*. Giving up or taking your own life will kill him. I don't even think the Mother will forgive you if you choose that path."

Like I didn't know that. I still nodded my understanding. At *Aore* Junae's last words, my mom started crying again. The room filled with the low boom of more than one person hitting the other side of the door. We could hear muffled voices, but the door was too thick to hear any words.

"Ajurelle, keep that door closed."

"Let them in!" my father called out. "You have no right to keep my mother out of this." But my dad didn't know for sure who was beyond that door. It could be the crowd from outside, demanding to get in and hear the verdict.

"Your sentence will be carried out now. Brendelin, bring Hallanevaë this way." *Aore* Junae held out his hand, turning to reveal the door in the far corner.

Brendelin rested his hands on my shoulders and guided me up to the dais. We followed *Loret* Maeson and Rassel as everyone's voices filled the room.

"We have this from here, Brendelin. Keep anyone from following us," *Aore* Junae said.

"Sir?"

"You heard me."

Brendelin looked down at me, brows furrowed. "Yes, sir." He turned back and stepped off the dais.

"Wait! Council members!" Cyaisn yelled as *Loret* Maeson pulled the door open.

The two members and Rassel pushed me through, and *Loret* Maeson shut the door as the pounding at the front of the room added to Cyaisn's demands to wait.

Rassel closed his eyes, breathing a deep, slow breath as the door closed. "Exile guarantees you will never come back. You are too dangerous and unpredictable to be trusted. It's a shame such talent is wasted on you. Such strength, and yet you can't control a bit of it. Such a shame."

"Yalu will never forgive any of you for this."

Rassel dropped his head, shaking it for a moment. "Then you shouldn't have killed your friends. They will all understand our logic later, even Zella. They're hurting now, but soon they'll come to terms with it. You will never be forgiven. Even your parents and Gileal will never forgive you, as soon as they calm down. They may even end up hating you, like Nolan does. For your sanity, consider everyone dead to you. As Nolan has said, you are dead to us. And honestly, the banishment? We have not been in contact with *Rosava* for a very long time. We don't know what awaits you over there."

"So, this is all a sham for them?"

"Some truths are too harsh for the general public. You would learn to understand this if we could have let you stay."

We walked single file down a narrow hall, Rassel behind me and the council members ahead of me, until we came to another door. Through there was the main hall of the Tree of Connection. We kept walking until we reached a dark corner, invisible from the rest of the hall.

"No one will see us here." Rassel checked around the corner again.

"Goodbye, Hallanevaë," *Loret* Maeson said as *Aore* Junae lifted a small gold *meril* up against the root.

"One question. If I don't have the *meril*, will it allow me to exit the other side?"

"We'll hold it to the tree long enough for you to go through." *Aore* Junae gestured for me to walk up to the portal.

I had no idea how this worked, as I'd never traveled through the Tree of Connection before. My heart thudded in my ears, racing in my chest. What if this didn't work? I was going to pass out. I looked back down the hall one last time.

Loret Maeson gave me a push to the edge. "Time to go, *savilë*." I didn't want to go. I wanted a fair trial and I wanted to say goodbye. "Walk straight through. It will only take three steps. One here, one in the middle, and one to exit."

"Wait..." Rassel clutched my arm where he'd held it before. "Your cuffs. You're no longer *Aeminan*, they're not yours." He reached for my left one and I flinched.

"Don't touch me." I jerked my arm out of his hand and with shaky hands I unhooked my third decade honor cuff from the top of my right ear.

Rassel held his hand out, but I sneered and gave it to *Aore* Junae.

"See to it that my grandmother gets this. She's waiting for it." I glared, hoping he believed Yalu knew *Aore* Junae had it.

"The other ones, too." Rassel glared.

I shook my head. Rassel went to grab for the cuffs. The cuffs Yalu and my parents gave me for my centennial birthday. The one An'di gave me because I really liked it. The one Nol gave me when—

Rassel grabbed my shoulder and squeezed until I cried out. My ear stung as he took my centennial ones. My lip curled at his smug face. I wanted to hurt him, shove him down and stomp on his heart like he was doing to mine.

"That's enough, Rassel."

"Nevie?" *Aore* Junae stepped between us. "Nevie, I'll get them to your family. I swear. Hand me the cuffs, child."

"You can't take them. I promised Nol—please?"

He continued to hold his hand out, but he didn't give me a smug attitude. "I'm sorry, but you are no longer *Aeminan*. If you want, I can give them back to Nolan."

"You can give them to us, or I'll make you."

"Rassel!" *Aore* Junae turned around, a deep frown set in his old face. Was he second-guessing his decision? "The cuffs, please?"

Crying, I unhooked the last part of my family.

"Check her pockets—"

"I swear, the Mother as my witness, if you speak one more time, Rassel, I will exile you as well."

"This is wrong and you know it," I whispered as I gave *Aore* Junae the remaining cuffs.

He pursed his lips and tugged on the pockets of my shirt before he turned me to face the tree and pressed on the small of my back. *Loret* Maeson held the *meril* to the wood that would take me into the unknown. I didn't fight it, but I didn't go easily either. Roots connected one entrance to the other—whether that was from realm to realm, place to place, or both, I did not know. The pull of *Endae* clung to me, but I needed to take that step or risk being stuck in this between realms place.

The step into the other realm felt like walking through a waterfall, at first a barrier, then a cold shock and pressure over my entire body. I shivered as I stepped into a cold, dark world. The pressure pushed me out of a much smaller tree. Not inside, or through the roots. The bark was too small to fit my hand between the rough vertical lines, only to my first finger joints.

The trees smelled different, sharp with wood smoke that stung my eyes. Not the gentleness that invited me to fill my lungs like home. Home...wasn't mine anymore. My eyes welled as I shivered in this frosty forest, my breath fogging around me.

"Laro?" My tears trailed down my face as I looked out into the lonely forest. "Murë?" I whispered. Drips of rain answered me. "Nol?" I dropped my face into my hands. My clothes snagged on the rough bark as I slid down the tree. I was alone.

I cried beside the tree, for my friends, my lost home, and me, but no one came. This was my fault. I chose to use the prank even though Twynolan warned me I didn't have the control for it. But what went wrong? I followed every instruction, measured and remeasured, wrote down and reviewed my notes. My personal, unpredictable family magic was the one thing that it could have been. I couldn't control it or keep it separate when I used traditional spells.

Clenching my hands into fists, I pressed them to my face and screamed into the night. The need to prove myself propelled me to take risks. I wanted to show them they were wrong about my magic. It wasn't a disability, and I wasn't a freak. But I was wrong, not them.

I screamed until my voice was hoarse. Then, shivering, I wrapped my arms around my legs and rested my chin on my knees to keep my heat in. I wiped my tears and stared at the leaf litter and dirt around me as I considered everything. Could I trust myself not to flaunt my magic? Would I use my magic morally? Responsibly?

The temptation to use it would always be there, and then what if it went wrong a second time? I could never use my magic again, not with the possibility of losing control. There had to be a way for me to take that temptation away.

My body naturally made the energy that it used to create magic. If I could block the organ responsible from sending out energy, then my body couldn't convert the energy into magic. Our healers always stressed the importance of maintaining a good flow of energy.

Closing my eyes and settling down on the cold, wet ground, I searched through my body for the system responsible for magic. My mind's eye found the core where my energy was converted. I followed it out into the cells that released my magic when I cast a spell.

As those cells began to constrict, pressure built as I imagined walls closing off the flow of magic. My body began to shake, waves of pain ebbed and flowed. The pressure grew, and the pain worsened. I couldn't give up, no matter how much this hurt. I could hear cells shrieking until I was just piercing pain, unable to sense anything else. With the closure of the last cells, I thought my heart stopped beating. My lungs seized and I passed out.

14

A CONSTANT DRIP OF water landing on my cheekbone woke me. The water rolled from there into my hair, eyes, and down my nose. My ears had collected water as well, the points serving as funnels into my ear canals. This place was nothing like the Tree of Communication. For one thing, I was outside. For another, the trees were so small I could see the dark clouds above me, and the rain was getting through everywhere.

My clothes were soaked, even my boots. My hair clung to my face and the weight pulled on my neck after I rolled over and pushed myself onto my elbows. I could hear nothing but the rain as it poured onto the forest floor, soaking the small leaves that were no bigger than my palm. Patches of snow scattered the ground between gaps in the trees. I felt like a giant.

Below me, the forest thickened—not dense, but if I spread my arms out, I could touch two trees. Every tree around me could fit into the Tree of Connection, with room to spare. The majority of the tree species were deciduous, their branches bare, and their brown, soggy leaves were long and came to a point at the top. Not a soul was here in this forest. So unlike home, I had no words. Home—*Endae* was not my home.

My stomach growled, drawing my attention back to myself instead of the shocking new world. I needed to find food and water soon. My hands were blue, and I realized I wasn't shaking. I moved to cast a warmth spell between my hands, but nothing happened. No magic.

This wouldn't be easy.

It took a while for my vision to adjust and level out when I stood up. The most logical way to start walking was down. But I knew better than to just ramble around the woods. I needed a compass, but I didn't have magic to make one. I was beginning to regret my choice to block my magic.

"This isn't going to work," I muttered, even as I marked a line in the dirt for reference in case I got turned around. I took a breath, let go of the tree, and followed the downhill slope to the next tree.

Ten trees away, my teeth started chattering, and I began to shake as my body started to warm with movement. The slope grew steeper, and I was doing all I could to pay attention to the next tree, the next mark on the ground, while trying to keep my shivering under control. The small trees were getting straggly and shorter.

There was a drop to the next trees. And another problem. Snow covered the area below me, hiding the true size of the drop. I sat with my feet dangling over the edge. I didn't spend a century climbing out Nol—Twynolan's windows and not learn how to scale a direct drop. So did he, but that didn't mean he was good at it. Hence, the ladder.

I almost smiled, felt my lips curve up, and then reality hit again. He'd disowned me, I'd killed my friends, and here I was in this odd...tiny tree world with the harsh biting smell of their trees and wood smoke. Rassel called it *Rosana*? *Rosave*? I couldn't remember. Ro-something.

I turned on my belly and slid, grasping the roots sticking out of the edge of the soil. My numb hands couldn't grip the root and I dropped, landing knee deep in snow. I couldn't feel anything, and I'd stopped shaking again. When had that happened? I waded through the snow to the tree I'd had my sights on earlier. There was no way to mark the ground in such deep snow. *Urro*!

Something moved ahead farther down the slope. Snow sliding? Branches? I hadn't seen one animal since I entered this realm. Not one. Down here, the snow muffled the sound of the rain. I needed to move. Would the moving thing harm me? All I needed was a forest dragon sneaking up on me. Did they have dragons here? Or just snow and trees and rain?

Keeping my eyes ahead, I dragged my numb legs through the snow. My brain started to register that the bright white area in front of me was a clearing. Another movement. Some sort of animal, slowly moving. It dipped its head to the snow. A darker shade of brown than the trees, it had a long neck, thin, long legs, and half the size of a mountain dragon. It had something on top of its head, too. Branches? Another one came out, smaller. Then another and another.

On my next step, I fell face-first and sank. Every time I pushed up, my hands went deeper. After a minute of fighting, I slowed down and lifted from the waist.

The animals were gone when I won the fight with the snow. I looked around, worried that they might ambush me, but at least there were other creatures here besides me. I considered that a positive, no matter if they were prey or predator.

By the time I made it to the tree line, I was ready to collapse from exhaustion, hunger, and thirst. Prints from the animals marred the smooth cover of snow, and beyond that...

"*Majut*." I clamped a hand over my mouth. No one was around to hear me swear. I could say whatever, whenever I wanted. Well, that word would take some practice to get used to. But the vast, far view of what lay before me deserved a strong word.

The clearing wasn't a clearing, but a road, winding down the side of the mountain. Past the road was a cliff and, out as far as I could see, trees like the ones I'd walked through all day. In the distance, they met orange and pink streaks stretching over the horizon. Under the setting sun, I squinted. Was that...Almost too small to make out, lines of smoke drifted up from houses below me. It was a village much smaller than *Rudairn*.

Even without snow, it would take hours—even a day—to get down to the village. And at night? But what else could I do? Jump off the cliff and hope I landed in a pile of soft snow? Two thin lines stretched out along the road in both directions. My heart leapt. Someone had to have made these tracks; they weren't natural.

They could come through before dark. Down the mountain road I went. With the easier, packed down snow, I made better time. But nothing could slow down the sun, and soon the only light came from the stars above me in the clear night sky. I stopped and looked for guidance. The faraway stars were unrecognizable. I truly was in a different realm.

I dropped to my knees, head hung low. I had no shelter and my body was numb. What did I do? The trees were dark shadows to my right, the valley was a dark abyss to my left, and I could get lost in the faint glow of the white snow. I was on the verge of crying when I heard something. Not the branches in the wind, but a male voice, like a "Ho, ho." Then two more. It came from behind me, up the mountain. Another "Ho, ho."

I needed to get off the road, but not too far. My legs weren't responding.

A yellow glow came from behind me and metal rhythmically clinked. Maybe it was what made the lines. I tried to pull myself out of the way, but my frozen, stubborn legs wouldn't budge as the glow came closer. There were other noises. Thumps and creaks. A dark shadow came around the corner, as large as a forest dragon, five times larger than me. The front of it moved, a quick up and down, followed by the thumping. Past that, the thing got wider. The light swung from side to side, unlike any light orb I'd ever seen.

A high, screeching animal voice, almost a sputter of noise, came out and then the "Ho, ho" again.

Gathering my courage, I waved my hands over my head and raised my voice. "*Oyi*!" My throat was rough and frozen. I tried again, but the pain in my throat kept my voice quiet. The thing continued on, closing in on me. Then the animal stopped, just out of my reach. It huffed, so close I could feel its warm breath.

From behind the animal, a voice—the one that was calling out—said something. A sentence, but I didn't understand, and my throat was too raw to answer. A darker figure jumped off with a crunch of snow. They brought the light—an unusual oval-shaped lantern with a yellow light globe. It swung as they walked around the large animal as it fidgeted and tutted.

They said something again, the voice deep like an *endao's*. A shorter phrase. "*Du vie ah tu.*" He said it again and pushed the light in my face. Not expecting that, I lifted my arms and covered my eyes. He repeated his words, and by this time I assumed it was a question.

I shook my head, squinting into his yellow lantern. He lowered his light, then he said something else. I shook my head again, tried to stand, and proceeded to fall.

His hand shot out and caught me. "*Vieya ahvehec ahmua.*" As he pulled on me, I got his meaning. He wanted me to come with him. He said something else I didn't catch, but he guided me up onto this wooden cart on wheels. The same kind that made the tracks. Now I felt stupid. I slipped on the step and watched my knee ram into the metal step but felt nothing.

Another, longer sentence, and then his arms went under my legs and on my back. He lifted me up and over the side and onto a bench seat at the front, with no arms to rest on or protect me from falling off. He rummaged around in the back, which was full of bags. He pulled out a blanket and laid it over my shoulders. Wouldn't it make more sense to cast a warming spell? He kept looking, clicked his tongue, and dug in the bag.

"Ah ha," he exclaimed as he popped back up, holding long pants and a long-sleeved shirt that would fall around my thighs. He held them up to the light and shook them. When I took them, he lowered the light closer to his face. His face was covered in hair! Hair that grew down to his chest and up to his ears and under his nose. His large red nose hung over it, and his eyes, while kind and worried, were small. Startled, I jumped back and almost fell out. Thankfully, he caught me.

He said something else and handed me the shirt again. This was no time for modesty. I stood and reached for the thick, scratchy shirt and climbed in the back. He sat on the bench with his back to me. The oblong buttons of my shirt, ones that my father had made, were cumbersome for my frozen fingers, but I managed. My clothes were almost frozen solid. I pulled his clothes on and tapped his shoulder. He turned, and I showed him that I was dressed. I pointed to the cart, hoping he'd understand that I felt safer back here where I wouldn't fall off.

He nodded and handed me the blanket I'd left on the bench. With another tutting hum sound, the animal started moving again, first slow, and then it picked up speed. I began to panic but reminded myself of the tracks on the road. He'd ridden this thing for a while and hadn't fallen. I needed to put my trust in him, or I'd die.

15

Far above, the purple and faint orange of sunrise glowed behind the mountains. We had hit every bump down the mountain that night. Every. Single. One. We finally arrived in the village I'd seen from above. The animal's feet must have something on them because they made a loud clomping noise as they stomped on the new surface. Heaps of snow shoved to the sides of the road exposed light-colored stones. I imagined the wooden wheels of the cart breaking at any moment—but they didn't.

The first buildings, on either side, were as tall as the Hall of Knowledge, but the stones weren't as well taken care of. The windows were arched, with bricks lining them. Some doors were also arched. Plants, tables, and chairs were set next to the buildings, and the roads were so narrow the cart just fit through. We went under two bridge-like walls, too narrow for anything to walk on, but sturdy enough to keep the buildings from toppling inward.

Around another corner, the smell of urine and feces assaulted my nose and lungs. I covered my mouth as the smell hurt my raw throat. The hairy *endao* made the animal stop with another noise. He climbed out to unhook long polls that attached it to the cart. Nodding to me, the *endao* pushed his palm away. Stay. He guided the animal into a room where the strong smell originated from. Why would someone put an animal in there? They needed fresh air, and someone should cast a thorough wash spell in there. Ten of them!

He came out of the building and opened the back of the cart. Too cold, nervous, and overwhelmed, I let him pick me up and set me on my feet. Thousands of hot knives stabbed my legs. I collapsed. I tried to stand again, but I'd demanded too much from my frozen legs and they wouldn't hold my weight. The *endao* settled the blanket more firmly on my shoulders and picked me up.

He carried me past one stone road and stopped at the first door of the next building. The door was a red so bright in the morning light, I had to cover my eyes. He stepped into a dark interior. Fear of the unknown darkness shuddered through me, but a moment later a fireplace grew from out of the darkness. Wood smoke filled the hot little room. Then a chair and another one. Two entrances on either side led to other darkened parts of this home. Real fire burned in glass sconces on the walls. The *endao* set me on the closest chair.

"Jean?" An *endaë's* quiet voice came from one of those entrances. Her thick dress reached the floor, and it had long sleeves with puffy shoulders and buttons from neck to waist. It looked more cumbersome than useful.

The one who brought me, Jean, said something to her.

She gasped. "*Non.*"

He seemed to ask a question, but she stared at me and didn't answer him. Her eyes squinted in the dim light. She leaned this way and that, as if a different angle would produce different results. She wasn't much taller than me, but she was more robust. She was older than my parents, judging by the lines along her pale lips and forehead. She kept her graying hair in a tight braid, rolled up some way on the back of her head. Her pale green eyes were bigger than the hairy *endao*.

The *endai* exchanged a short phrase. She set her hands on her hips, looked at me, and shook her head. Shaking meant negation, it had to. "*Non.*"

He thrust his hand out toward me and argued. Again, she shook her head. She wasn't going to let me stay. Could she at least let me get warm? She stepped close and inspected my face again. With pursed lips, her nose flared. "*Wun nuit!*" She held up one finger and stormed out.

The *endaë* came back with a cup in her hands, telling Jean something that seemed like scolding. They both looked at me, their eyes as wide as they could get. Then the *endaë* smiled and handed me the warm cup.

With a dip of my head in gratitude, I took a sip. Knives sliced, sharper than the ones in my legs, piercing the inside of my throat.

My cup was taken from me and someone patted my back until my throat stopped burning. Jean left the room and came back with another cup. The *endaë* handed me the new one and I took a hesitant sip. It still hurt, but this one had a sweetener that soothed my throat. Jean left after a few sips into the second cup. The *endaë* would walk in and out of the room, checking on me and clanking things in another room until I smelled food cooking. The next time she came through, she pulled the blanket off me and exchanged it for warm one.

Not long after that I heard steps from the side where my hairy savior had gone. Jean came into the firelight. "*Tout bon?*" he asked as if I understood. After a curt nod of self-satisfaction, he headed to the room where the *endaë* was working.

Another set of footsteps, lighter than his, came from the back and another *enda* came in. An older boy, possibly my age. Theirs? His dark brown eyes were brighter than his father's, but the same color. Freckles were scattered over the bridge of his nose. He adjusted a strap holding his pants up as he stared at me.

The *endaë* walked toward the boy as he stared, blinking and probably still half-asleep. She made him lean over so she could kiss his cheek. Yep, his mother.

"*Cie es?*" he asked, rubbing his neck.

"*El nes pe son.*" She waved me away, like she wanted him to ignore me.

His lips bunched up, but she shooed him toward the smell of food. All thoughts of me were forgotten. The mother came back in and handed me a plate with soft scrambled eggs on a slice of herb bread. I nodded to her in thanks. After breakfast, the father and son left and she sat down in front of me.

"*Cheveux.*" She pointed to my hair. I stared, she paused. I figured out the word—I didn't want to say it with my raw throat.

After the pause continued, I swallowed and tried to copy the word. "*Savu.*" Not good. I wasn't sure if I could make that hissing, slurring sound with a nasal "uh" at the end. For someone fluent in two other languages, I expected more understanding from myself. Or maybe I was just burned out.

She licked her lips and got up, on a mission as she stormed out. But she came back in with long black ribbons, not looking offended at all. She held the ribbons to her hair, spoke like I knew the language, and handed them to me.

I nodded and lifted them to my own hair, which pleased her. Then she revealed a wooden stick with bristles on one end. She sat down in front of me and undid her own hair, letting it tumble down her shoulders as it untwisted.

"*Brosse tes cheveux,*" she explained. "*Brosse.*" She held up the bristled stick and moved it through her hair. Like a comb but pokier.

"*Bros,*" I croaked.

"*Brosse,*" she corrected. I repeated until she was satisfied. Then came the other word. Oh boy.

I swallowed, my throat in shreds, and repeated the next word for the twelfth time in a row. "*Cheveux.*"

"*Oui!*" Yes.

So glad she approved. I hoped she wouldn't make me say more.

"*Brossez-vous les cheveux avec la bross.*" She didn't make me repeat her as she kept going. She parted her thick hair on either side and picked one part up at the very top. Then she took a ribbon and proceeded to plait her hair in a complicated six-sectioned braid, using the ribbon to tie it off.

She touched the side of my head, above my ear, then the side of hers where the braid covered hers. Then she lifted her hair and pointed at the tip of her ear. She patted my hair and covered my ears with it. Why would she want me to cover my ears?

We practiced her complicated braid, first her hair, then mine. If I didn't make them tight enough, she made me redo it, an endless feat. My stiff fingers ached, and I just couldn't get the braids tight enough with them. Sometime much later, her son and companion came home. She checked the sides of my ears as my hairy savior called out.

"*Bonjour,* Marie."

Marie, huh? She could have told me at any time.

"*Bonjour, Jean et André.*" She went over and kissed their cheeks.

I had more names. Jean, my hairy savior of the bright red nose. André followed, a large, toothy grin on his face. Marie pulled both of them over and made her son turn, so I could see his ear. One could hardly call them pointed. Jean, her companion, or possibly husband, grumbled, but Marie brought him in front of me as well. She took off his hat and showed me his ears. I startled and jumped in my seat. His ears were round. No tips. How did he wear cuffs? Considering that, where were their marriage cuffs?

"*Oui.*" Marie nodded, then covered her normal tipped ears again. Marie met her family's eyes and shooed them to the kitchen.

Marie sat in front of me again and raised her eyebrows. She pointed at herself. "*Fée et humain.*" She pointed in the direction where Jean and André had just gone. "*Jean est humain. Mon fils, André, est en partie une fée.*" Marie pressed her hand to my knee. "*Tu es un elfe.*" I looked from Marie to where her family had walked to. She licked her lips and lowered her voice. "*Endaen.*" She pointed to me. Finally, a word I knew!

"*Ja!*"

Marie held a finger to her lips. "*Non endaen.*" She sliced her hand in the air. "*Non fée.*" She pointed to herself, then her family. "*Fée et humain.*"

Urro, we were different species!

"*Non endaen,*" I said, repeating her quiet words, then waved my hand around the room. There were no *endai* here. "*Non fée.*" Only her, *fée* and *humain*. I understood. We were alone in our different species. But then where were her people?

"*Fée non Endae.*" I hated to disappoint her, but if she was looking for her kin, she wouldn't find it there.

"*Je sais.*" She patted my knee, then leaned on it to stand. "*Je sais.*"

"Maman?" André came up behind her.

They exchanged words. André gestured at me, then my hair. She frowned. André left the room, his footsteps thundering down to wherever he'd come from this morning. A moment later, he returned and shook a piece of taupe-colored cloth bunched in his fist.

"Oh, *oui*!" Marie took the cloth from her son and shook it out. It was a rectangle long enough to tie around my head several times. Marie covered her ears, then pointed at me and then at the cloth.

Marie demonstrated how to wear it. I practiced and practiced until Marie approved and it didn't feel like it would fall off.

After our next meal, Marie brought me back into a room. She laid a set of clothes, similar to what she wore, on the bed. I gulped. The clothing was dark brown with cloth-covered buttons down the middle and at the ends of the sleeves. It turned out I had to wear two tops. One hard strap with strings underneath and then the loose fitting one tucked into skirts—yes plural, which were also tied together with a leather strap and metal buckle.

How did they walk with these things on? I couldn't bend over, and I couldn't step without my foot getting caught in the fabric. The oddest things I would ever considered learning. After another fall during my walking lessons, Marie couldn't hold in her laugh. I knew she'd been holding it in. I was a spectacle. With a hiccup and a gasp, I stopped laughing. This was the first time I'd laughed since...I tried to keep my eyes dry, I tried to obey myself. But I missed my parents, and Twynolan. I hadn't seen Yalu in a week. What would I have given to hug An'di properly. When was the last time I'd told my mom I loved her?

Marie touched my hand as I wiped at my tears. "*Ta maman te manque?*"

Maman—what André called her. My tears disobeyed me. I covered my face. Marie's arms wrapped around me and rubbed my back until my crying subsided.

"*Tu pleures.*" She pressed her finger to my chest, then frowned and traced her face like following a tear. I cried, yes. She squeezed my shoulder and nodded, then placed her hands, palms out, in front of me. Stop. She sat up tall and placed her hand over her heart, giving herself a few pats as she held her chin high. I might be sad and miss my parents, but I needed to be strong. If I wanted to survive, I needed to do this and wear uncomfortable clothing and hide my ears. I could do that, because like Marie tried to tell me, I needed to be strong.

16

ANDRÉ HANDED ME A pail of grain outside the next morning. He guided me over to the large animal that pulled the cart last night.

"*Comme ça.*" André grabbed my hands and lifted the pail.

The beast towered over me. André only came up to its eyes. But the oddest thing was its feet. Instead of toes, each leg had one big round foot with a hard outer shell.

"*Nourris-la.*" André shook the pail, encouraging me to feed it. The animal, which had a long face, nudged the pail with its large nostrils and eased the pail over before dipping its mouth in. "*Jumont.*" André patted its neck.

"*Jumon,*" I repeated.

André laughed and shook his head. "*Non—*"

"André!" Jean snapped at his son as he stood beside the cart, ending our impromptu lesson. André jumped into the cart and grabbed a bag his father handed up to him. Jean tossed up three more and André placed them near the front of the cart.

Marie walked over, holding a bundle of cloth. "*Ma chère?*" She pushed the bundle in my arms. "*Le vôtre.*"

The thing had some weight to it. I squeezed and felt stiff handles. A bag? I let the bottom go and opened the top to find my clothes folded inside. "*Perudara—*" Thank—

"*Non—*" She covered her mouth and pressed a finger to my chest with her other hand. "*Non endaen. Non.*" So, no speaking *Aemirin*? Marie began fretting, touching my clothes, my scarf, the bag, and at last my hands. With tears in her eyes, she spoke to me like I understood her.

"Marie." Jean's grumble sealed her lips.

She stared, her wide eyes brimming with tears. "*Tu dois être courageuse maintenant.*" She shook my hands, the heavy bag swaying. "*Soit courageuse.*"

I nodded.

"*Prête?*" André said from inside the cart. "*A demain*, Maman." André held his hand out to me.

I gave him a flat look and gestured at my new skirts. Marie laughed.

André scratched his head and chuckled. He hopped down and lifted me over the side. With a tissue to her eyes, Marie waved goodbye, standing on her doorstep.

Jean didn't go as fast as before, but then I wasn't hypothermic anymore either. Brush and small trees hid the cliffside mere feet away for most of the travel down the mountain. The road wound its way down the mountain, turning back and forth and back again, until I was dizzy.

Every village had the same bright orange roofs and smooth stone walls closing in on each side of us, so close I wondered if the cart would fit. Ages and ages later—my butt was sore even through the layers of clothing—we rounded a curve, absent of any trees, revealing the magnificent view of below.

A valley sprinkled with snow. Like Mother Anara herself laid a blanket over the world and sprinkled it with flour. Bushes and trees poked out of that blanket, some skeleton branches reaching to the sky. Small evergreens looked like they were wearing a coat of white.

"*Regarder.*" André waved out to the landscape. "*Village.*" Beyond, past the valley, a sea of orange roofs spread out in the distance, with a dark gray expanse behind it—water? Not just water, an ocean. I inhaled the air, hoping to smell the sea on the breeze, but we were still too far away.

As day turned into dusk and dusk turned to night, we made our way down the mountain and closer to the city by the sea. All my excitement, built up from André's own excitement, withered as Jean's horse pulled up to the buildings. This place that André had shown me, the vast city near the sea, held no wonder for me once we arrived. I wished nothing more than to turn around where we could smell fresh air. The only smell of the sea I could pick out was rotten. I did not want to see the beach. What in the realms did they do to this place?

The horse's round feet clomped on the empty, muck-filled streets. No one seemed to pick up any of these animals' feces; they just swept them to the edges. How would I walk in this outfit without getting my skirts filthy?

Jean stopped the cart in front of a large white building, almost as large as the Hall of Knowledge.

"*Prête*?" André said, the same word as before. He jumped down and held his hands out to me, waiting.

I shook my head. "*Seta quineta duwano.*" *This place is filthy.* "I'll get my skirts dirty." And perhaps more—if the smell was any indication. I shook the bottom of my dress to show them what I meant.

They weren't getting it. "Screw it." I jumped, holding my skirts as high as I could. My landing didn't squelch. I took that as a win, but my boots left indentations on the muddy stones as I followed André and Jean to the building.

The entrance was in the center with three white, two-story-high pillars to each side and arched windows on the second floor. André held the tall wooden doors open. The shiny wood floors creaked as we stepped through the entrance. Paintings of frowning, serious people lined the walls. Lanterns, similar to those at Marie and Jean's house, but larger, hung in pairs close to the walls.

"*Bonjour!*" A female's voice echoed through the hall, followed by clacking, as if the woman wore shoes made of wood. They did not sound comfortable. She wore her gray hair in the same way Marie wore her hair. She seemed nice; maybe it wouldn't be so bad here—if I never stepped outside. As Jean and the female spoke, her expression turned sour and her words grew clipped. Or not so nice.

With a final, frustrated sigh, she looked me up and down. "*Quel est ton nom?*" Her voice echoed through the hall.

I jumped back, startled by the volume of her voice. Yes, that would make me understand her. I shook my head. Jean implored to the elder, pointing to me and then to the three of them. She huffed again and pulled down her stiff shirt.

"*Suis-moi.*" She waved her hand and walked back the way she came, her shoes clacking on the hard floor.

André whispered something to his father, but we followed her to her workroom at the end. She handed Jean some papers and glared at him while he wrote on them. He handed them back, the elder checked them, set them on the table, and looked at me.

"*Suis-moi,*" she said again.

I pulled my savior in for a fierce hug, as tight as I could, then a briefer, yet just as tight one for André. The elder snapped something harsh and André pushed me toward her.

"*Au revoir.*" *Goodbye.* André cleared his throat and Jean nodded before the elder snapped again. I hurried behind, waving with tears in my eyes.

The banister on the stairs wiggled and groaned as the elder held it in one hand while grabbing her skirts with the other. I'd just hold my skirts and not put my trust in a groaning, possibly hazardous banister. She kept up a clipped and irritated commentary as we walked up to a third floor.

She led me down to the end of the hall and waved for me to go in a room. Rows of beds on either side, each one with its own lump covered in blankets. One lump moved, a head lifted, woken up by the noise of the elder's loud shoes. Another head lifted and then more as the elder walked me through the room to the first empty bed. If my count was correct, there were twenty-five beds in the room, and three beds in total weren't occupied.

She pointed at the first empty bed. "*Rendormir.*"

Each head fell back to their bed the moment the word left her lips. I chose to listen and follow her directions, even if I didn't understand the words. The meaning was more than clear. I was in bed and covered before she clattered back down the hall, but as soon as the door slammed shut, every one of them sat up, whispering to one another and looking down the rows to me.

The one beside me, even littler than the first person, whispered something to me. I rolled over and covered my head with the blanket. My lip trembled, and I squeezed my eyes shut as the children whispered.

17

THE SLAP OF BROWN-GRAY water hitting the *pavé* in the back of the *orphelinat* didn't stink nearly as bad as the pails Natalie threw out here this morning with the feces of the building's inhabitants. But the dirty mop water pushed the feces that clung to the middle of the small alley to the sides.

My first few weeks at this place was spent in this manner: learning chores and learning their language from the children. Madame Allard, the elder, I didn't trust yet, and she was always in such a sour mood! The first few days of my chores I'd vomited so much, Natalie had to take over—the only other girl my age. I couldn't understand how these people hadn't built some sort of sewage system in their humongous stone city. All of this waste was pushed out into the stormwater and into their bays. But we were the oldest and she welcomed my assistance with the tougher chores and assistance with the youngsters. Even if I couldn't handle a "little" feces.

"Natalie?" A little voice spoke out from behind us. Aimée tugged on Natalie's skirts. "Matthieu is hurt," Aimée asked in French.

"*Ce qui s'est passé?*" *What happened*? Matthieu was one of the more dramatic of the thirty-one boys.

Aimée shrugged. "*Je ne sais pas.*" *I don't know.* Then she explained more in words I hadn't learned yet. They got Natalie hurrying, so it wasn't just drama this time.

As we got to the bottom of the stairs, Matthieu was sitting up, blood flowing out his nose and down his arm. "Owie," the boy cried.

"Yes, I can see that. Did you fall?"

The boy shook his head and looked at the banister. Natalie growled and went on a little torrent. She made him stand and then walked him into their small infirmary. I walked to the front of the building and stood at the window.

I leaned in close and listened to the happenings of the busy city. Five children, all varying in sizes, followed a woman as she bustled down the street—likely their mother. The littlest half ran, half stumbled against the boy ahead of her as he dragged her forward. These people always seemed to have some place to be and were frantic to get there.

There were two types of people. Ones with the simple outfits were what Natalie called *locale*, and the others—the ones with the silk and lace dresses and walking sticks—were *touristes* who came in winter. I stared out the window watching the people, the carts, and the horses. So many children walking with parents, although, I didn't see many elders.

"Fille," Natalie called from the infirmary. "We have work to do."

I looked around at the spotless orphanage, then back out to the busy world. She was right, however. All the others had to work; I needed to do my fair share. I was learning quite a bit here, in this place people brought unwanted or parentless children.

"I know you are curious, but Madame Allard will be angry if we don't work when it isn't free time," she told me as she handed me a broom and headed toward the closet to drop off the pail.

I nodded, unable to speak here. Marie warned me to stay quiet, and I would, except with the children. None of the adults heard me speak, nor did they ask me to say anything. They just scolded. No one asked why I didn't talk, and no one tried to take away my scarves. They didn't ask me my name, choosing to call me girl—*Fille*. It was just as well; I didn't feel right using Hallanevaë or any form tied to my old life.

"Natalie!" Madame Allard called, standing in the main hall. "*Venez ici, maintenant!*" *Come here now.* Then she pointed at me. "*Améne-la avec toi.*"

Natalie set the pail down and started running. "Come, Fille!"

Two adult heads turned upon our entrance. A robust female, a head taller than me, wore a blue-and-white striped skirt and dark blue top.

Lace peaked out of the cuffs of her long sleeves and low neckline. While taller than my grandmother, her gray-and-black hair reminded me of her. The man stood opposite her, taller, with a tall stiff hat and dark hair under his nose. His long black coat hid much of his clothes, but his shoes were shiny and black—underneath the spots of dirt from outside.

"Madame?"

Madame Allard snapped her fingers and pointed at two spots in the middle of the room for us to stand. Natalie fidgeted beside me, brushed her hands down her stained dress, and then tugged her thick brown braids. I stayed still and clasped one wrist with the other hand. The man tapped his walking stick on the floor and paced around us, assessing us as he asked Madame questions I didn't understand.

Madame responded mostly in the positive. One question made Natalie start and Madame gave him a harsh, offended *non*.

"*Tui.*" The man poked his stick at me. "What is your name?"

"Monsieur, the girl doesn't understand French."

The man scoffed at Madame Allard and shook his head. He pointed to Natalie. "*Ensuite tu feras.*" *Then you will do.*

Natalie gasped. "Madame? Where am I going?"

"*An usine.*" Madame continued, too fast for me to follow. Natalie's eyes grew wide the more Madame explained.

"Fille." Madame's clipped tone drew my attention away from Natalie. But Madame wasn't talking to me, she was talking to the large woman. After a few moments' conversation, the woman came forward and inspected me. She reached for my arm and I flinched. Why would she touch me?

The woman asked me a question, and Madame reminded her I couldn't speak French. She rolled her eyes, but she had her back to Madame, so Madame couldn't see the smile on her lips. I liked her smile.

The new woman plucked something out of her big bag. A tiny cushion of sorts. She pulled a thin metal pin with a thread attached to it out of the cushion. She held it up. "Do you know what this is?"

I reached out and took the needle from her. Wennië always had a bit of sewing to do with her fabric dying. I nodded. She smiled again and turned to face Madame. "*Ella fera.*"

Madame waved us away with a few words to Natalie, who clasped my hand and pulled me to the stairs.

By the time we made it to the third floor I was out of breath. "What is happening?"

"We are going into *le programme de travail*."

"What is that?"

"Where older orphans go work and become adults."

"Like a school?"

"*Non*, we are going to work. Petre and Phillipe will turn *douze ans* soon, then they will leave, too."

"What is *douze ans*?"

Natalie stopped inside the girls' room. "*Douze.*" She counted to twelve on her fingers.

"*Ah, oui.*" Twelve decades.

"*Ans*...times around the sun."

I stumbled in the hall. "*Ans?*" I held my finger up. "Around the sun?" Not decades?

"*Oui*. What is the problem?"

Oh no. I tried to get my throat to unstick, but the shock that these people counted their age in years and not centuries was too much to process. I shook my head and forced my brain to work. "*Non. Douze ans.* I understand."

She patted my shoulder when we got to the girls' room. "Good, now go get your things. We're leaving."

I ran to my bed and threw the few belongings I owned into the bag Marie had given me.

One of the girls cleaning the room stopped and looked at Natalie. "Leaving?"

"Yes, Celeste." Natalie patted her on the head. "We must hurry. Madame is in a mood." And Natalie wasn't exaggerating. Madame waited at the front door with the two visitors that we'd be leaving with. My head was full of questions, but everything went so fast.

"*Viens.*" *Come.* The woman waved her hand.

But before Natalie or I could get out the door, a roll of thunder came from the stairs, along with children's voices.

Six or seven of them came up and wrapped their arms around Natalie. Two youngsters came to me. "Natalie, Fille!" they cried.

"We'll miss you!"

"Don't go!"

"I want to come with you!"

And more children buzzed in a swarm of high voices. Madame barked, demanding them to go back to their chores, but gave up after a minute. Both the man and Madame's faces were red in anger, while the woman in the striped skirt just laughed.

"Let them say goodbye." The woman I was going with waved to the children. "Fille, *Poursuivre*!" That was all I needed to bend down and hug as many crying little ones as possible.

"Go. Now." Madame clapped her hands after a count of ten. "You made your farewells. Back to your work, children," She snapped and started walking away in a *panique*, as Natalie called it whenever Madame got worked up and irritated. She didn't even say a goodbye.

"*Viens*, Fille," Natalie called back from the open front door, waiting for me.

She engulfed me in a fierce hug as soon as we were both outside. We shivered in the chilly winter air. The new dress the orphanage had gifted me was nowhere near new and not cold weather appropriate. All the girls wore higher skirts and looser tops. While they were still cumbersome, at least I wasn't tripping with every step.

"Take care of yourself and good luck." With that, before I could say anything, Natalie ran after the man.

The woman in stripes turned to me. "*Prête*?" *Ready*?

I nodded and followed her into the city. Thanks to a storm that lasted for two days, the air didn't sting my nose, since there was only a day's worth of excrement on the streets.

"My name is Josephine. My shop is very small, but with *l'afflux de clients* I have been having, I need an assistant. Do you understand?"

I squinted as I tipped my head side to side. Neither a nod or a shake.

"Eh, you'll learn more. *Citoyens de la classe supérieure* use my services for the most part. Do you have nicer clothes in the bag?"

I shook my head again.

"Do you have more shoes?"

She wrinkled her nose when I shook my head a third time. Would she make me wear different shoes? *Please, Mother, no.* All the boots at the orphanage were stiff and uncomfortable. My boots had a good deal of time left in them because of my father's spell to keep the leather clean and supple.

Josephine stopped and turned to face the road. "Take my hand. We're crossing the street."

My stomach dropped. How? With all the people and horses clomping up and down? What if we got separated? I couldn't tell one stone building from another. They all had the same tall branchless trees planted in front with their long, stiff leaves at the top. This place was crazy and she wanted to cross the street in a random area? We weren't even at a crossroads.

Josephine looked up and down the street. Then, when there was a small gap, she broke out into a run, dragging me with her. I tripped on a larger stone and Josephine stumbled. A horse reared back, letting out a shrill scream that I'd only heard them use a few times. It was almost upon us. Josephine tugged, and we kept running, making it to the other side without any more incidents.

Josephine bent over, her hands on her thighs, as she gasped for breath. After counting to one hundred, I placed my hand on her back, trying to express without words my concern for her well-being.

"Je vais bien. Juste essoufflé." *I am fine,* she said between gasps. The other sentence was new. After several more heartbeats, she stood. "Let's go."

We left the rush and noise behind, enough that I could hear her footsteps. My boots weren't as noisy as the stiff, uncomfortable ones humans wore.

Around the next corner, I stopped and couldn't take another step at the sight before me. A lane of trees went down in the middle of the road. While small, they had branches and leaves that rustled in the wind, unlike the odd ones planted everywhere else in this lifeless stone city.

Josephine tugged on my arm. *"Tôt va bien?"* *Are you well?*

I nodded and inhaled through my mouth for the first time during our walk. No, not any cleaner, but at least I could hear the leaves rustling in the wind. Josephine waited until I was ready before continuing down the tree abundant lane.

"We're here!" Josephine claimed, drawing my attention away from the lane of trees. A pink-and-white striped fabric hung above the top of the entrance. She pulled out a ring of small metal sticks with pointy teeth and shoved one in a hole in the door. It rotated ninety degrees before she pushed the door open and bumped a bell above to make a delightful jingle.

I couldn't help but smile. I stopped. Was this the first time I'd smiled since, no, but, then I realized they couldn't smile anymore…Tears threatened to spill, but I wiped them away. Tears were selfish, and I wouldn't wallow in self-pity. I didn't deserve that.

"*Très bien*?" *All right*? Josephine asked, bringing me out of my thoughts.

I nodded and followed her into her place, where I'd live for who knew how long. If they lived much shorter lives, I wouldn't be staying here that long. But this was no time for questions, as more immediate things needed attention. Like listening to Josephine's instructions and learning where I'd sleep and what my days would be like from now on. Busy and simple.

18

A MONTH WENT BY in a cloud of depression. Josephine asked questions about everything, but I didn't fall behind in my duties, and I didn't let it interfere with what she required of me.

She asked if was I upset about losing my parents? Yes.

Did I remember more about the accident? Yes.

Did I want to talk about my nightmares? No.

She offered to listen when I was ready. I gave her a thankful nod and went about my days, learning more of their language as I tried to follow her conversations with her customers. I even spoke a few words to Josephine. Not many, though. Yes, no, thank you. A few others.

I missed home, and I couldn't keep the tears away at night. I cried for home and my parents, for my friends and Twynolan. That brought on a new thought, the memory of what he'd said. Our bond couldn't really break, not our souls' connection, but the friendship between us in this life had. If I was going to move on, I had to cope with the loss. Was mourning a loved one selfish? Perhaps. But I lied to myself and said it wasn't, that it was natural. I allowed myself to mourn everyone at home, for while they lived, I'd died to them.

"How do you get these clothes so clean, Fille?"

I shrugged. By not using a pool—what they called *lavoirs*—when the rest of the women used them. I found going early mornings and late evenings was enough time for the natural spring underneath to filter the dirt from the other women's laundry.

Josephine tugged at the end of my braid and took the clean dress to the front, where it would wait for its owner. She hummed as she hung the dress up, then busied herself around the front of the shop. Before long, I stopped watching her and got back to my duties.

"Fille? Would you go upstairs and fetch more chalk? I must have taken the bag upstairs."

"*Oui*, Josephine."

I hurried up the back steps. Josephine had placed a parcel down on a chair near the little fireplace last night while I was sewing…Nothing was there. Of course! The small table next to her bed. I found the parcel, swiped it up, and hurried back down.

About halfway down, I heard a high-pitched voice, higher than I normally heard here. Children didn't usually come into Josephine's shop. "*Maman, s'il te plaît, s'il te plaît emmène-moi au parc après ça!*" Mama, please, please take me to the park after this!"

I peeked around the corner at the bottom of the stairs to listen to the mother's exasperated reply. The girl must have been asking her mother for a while, as the mother's French was almost too fast for my brain to translate. Her eyes widened as she looked at Madame Josephine from across the counter. "Emmaline, not today. Stop pestering me, or we won't go at all."

The woman held a bag in front of her while the girl—Emmaline—stood beside her, now resolved to not "pester" her. She didn't look older than Natalie. To think this girl was probably only ten or eleven years old! Astonishing.

Her dress was the same length as mine, around her shins, but everything she wore was white and light blue—the same color of Twynolan's eyes. My sharp intake of breath brought all three females's attention to my hiding place, and I had to give up and come out, carrying the parcel of chalk to Josephine. I ducked my head and went to hide in my little room of projects that needed to be done by tomorrow.

Their conversation picked back up after I hid around the corner of my workspace, but the girl—with her white-and-blue dress and white stockings and her hair!—I knew she watched me, I caught the flash of auburn a few times when I looked up. Her hair was an auburn darker than An'di's, but not by much. She wore it in a braid, similar to mine, except she had a white bow in the back and a daisy clip at the temple.

"Emma, time to go!"

"*Un moment, maman.*" She sounded closer than I thought she was.

I snuck over and poked my head around the wall to come face-to-face with the girl. We both gasped and reared back. Emma caught the table next to her, but my fingers slipped when I tried to grab the wall. My head hit something behind me, which in turn fell—it was the mannequin and the dress jacket hanging on it. I spun on my hands and knees to catch it before it hit the floor, but only managed to stumble and land on top of it.

"Fille!" Josephine gasped. Her footsteps grew louder, and I tried to untangle myself from the mess I'd made.

Hands were pulling on me, and someone grabbed the mannequin and the chair that managed to topple over as well. That's when I saw Emma picking up the thimbles, needles, and thread that had fallen out of my sewing kit. Someone wrapped their arms around my middle and pulled.

"Let me see. Are you injured?" Josephine checked me all over. "Not a scratch."

"*Je suis désolé,* Josephine." *I'm sorry,* Josephine.

"Don't fret." She patted my shoulder and leaned on her arms to stand.

"Is she all right?" Emma asked.

"I believe so."

Emma came over and crouched in front of me, pressing her skirts down and wrapping her arms around her knees. She touched my cheek and smiled. I swallowed, still embarrassed with myself and the situation that I'd created. "*Bonjour, je suis Emma.*" *Hello, I am Emma.* "It's nice to meet your acquaintance. What is your name?"

"Fille is shy and is still learning our language. I was told she lost her family in the mountains. A tragic event. Isn't that right, Fille?"

"But you call her girl?" Emma wrinkled her nose.

"Until she can remember her name, yes."

"Enough questions, Emmaline. Let's leave them alone to get her settled down."

"Maman, can she come to the park with us?"

"Emmaline—"

"*S'il te plaît, maman.*" *Please, Mama.* "Maybe all she needs is a friend."

I hung my head. That wasn't what I was here for. Neither of the adults spoke during this awkward moment. Perhaps children didn't understand how orphans were placed.

"Fille is my...er...apprentice. She has to work for the day."

"But..." Emma stopped tugging on her mother. "Can't we go to the park when she's not working? She must quit working some time."

"*Ma puce...*"

Josephine helped me off the floor. She wiped her hands on her apron. I settled my skirts.

Emma's mother looked down at me, then at Josephine. "Perhaps an arrangement can be made?"

Josephine placed a hand on her chest. "*Pardon, madame?*" Her face grew redder by the second as she waited for the mother to respond.

"Emma, go stand by the door. I must talk to Madame Josie."

Emma huffed. "I just wanted a friend." She pouted as she stomped away.

"*J'ai un problème.*" *I have a problem.* And like most adults here, she started speaking too fast for me to follow.

"I suppose that I could spare her for a few hours..." Josephine said, her words always slow enough for me to translate.

The women stared down at me with similar contemplative expressions on their faces.

"Fille? Would you be willing to take Emma to the park this evening? After your chores are finished?" Josephine spoke slowly as this was quite a longer sentence than I was used to.

"My Emma wants to go." The mother waved her arm around as she explained. "But none of her siblings nor her father or I have time tonight."

Were they joking? Why didn't they just come out and say that I could play with Emma after work? Then I realized, they thought I was twelve. But Josephine knew I was smart. She had to know I saw past this. Josephine shrugged with a lopsided smile.

"Do you understand?"

I smiled. "*Oui*, Josephine, *madame*,"

"*Vous irez?*" *You'll go?*

"*Oui.*"

"Settled," Emma's mother said. "Have her come to our apartment around six then?"

"She's not used to navigating the city," Josephine said. "Once I sent her to get bread and Monsieur Jacque found her blocks away."

"Ah, then I'll send my oldest with Emma for the trade. Certainly, they can find their way back here? It's straight down the lane."

"They should. Once lamps are lit, then you head back home. Understand, Fille?"

"*Oui*, Josephine." That was easy enough to do. I was so excited, I was bouncing on my toes. "Um..." I pointed to my work.

"Yes, get started."

Right after cleaning the dishes, I ran down and waited for Emma outside the door. The lamps wouldn't be lit for two hours still. Not many people were out, mostly men and a few couples. The carriages—with their horses—were far fewer as well.

At last, Emma stepped around the corner, skipping beside a much taller boy with wild brown hair that fell to just below his ears. That must be the older brother. He had his hands shoved in the pockets of his pants, the same kind of straps over his shoulders as Jean and André had worn. He wore a nice white shirt and had a jacket—either brown or black—slipped over his arm.

Emma wore darker stockings, black boots, and a brown dress—a much simpler one than she wore earlier. As the pair came closer, perhaps two shops away, the boy slowed down. After a few hops, Emma stopped and waited for him.

"Come on, Gabe." Emma's voice echoed through the empty block.

"I'm coming, I'm coming." He leaned forward as if to hurry but then dragged his feet.

"Ugh! Gabriel." Emma grabbed his arm and yanked, only to be pulled in and leaned against.

"I can't walk any farther, sister. Carry me!"

"Gabriel! Stop." He reminded me of An'di, with his teasing.

They both turned as I approached instead of waiting. *"Bonjour."* I wrung my hands and kept my voice low.

Emma tugged on her brother, much like she had with her mother. "Do you feel it, Gabe? Do you?"

Gabe stared down at me with a blank face and wide eyes. *"Oui."*

Emma jumped in a little circle, her skirt fluttering with her movements. "I told you! Maman feels it, too."

"Did—did I do something wrong?"

"Aha." Emma clapped. "I knew you could talk."

I backed away. She was going to tell!

"Non—non." Gabe held his hand out. *"Merde,* Emma, you scared her."

I stepped back.

"You didn't do anything wrong. Promise. Emmaline is just excited because she had a feeling you...could say more. She won't tell if you don't want the adults to know."

But was he an adult? "I won't tell either. You're safe."

"What—then, what are you talking about? What do you feel?"

"You're different." Emma shrugged, as if that explained everything.

I blinked, waiting for more. When she didn't elaborate, I looked at Gabe. "Care to—eh—say more?"

"Here, let's walk."

"But your mother...um, wanted me to take her."

He looked so crestfallen by the idea. "I have some free time, just to walk with you a bit. Unless...you mind?"

"No, come, if you want to."

Gabe stood up straight, pushed his shoulders back, and began loping down the lane. *"Bien."* He smirked.

Emma giggled. "You must be careful with Gabe, or he'll guilt you into doing just about anything." She hooked her arm in mine and hurried us after her brother. Emma and I were the exact same height. And I'd noticed she acted older with no adults around.

"How old are you?" I asked Emma.

"Ten—"

"Not yet." Gabe stuck up a finger.

"In three months." She rolled her eyes, then stuck her tongue out at him. "*Ugh, incorrigible.*"

"You sound like Maman."

"Well, Maman is right."

I laughed at their banter, so natural, warm, and familiar. I missed bickering with An'di and Twynolan.

"Why are you sad?" Emma whispered.

"*Moi?*"

"Yes, you."

"I...I can't talk about it."

"Hmm." Emma watched our feet, stepping in unison, again reminding me of Twynolan. I looked at the shops.

"What is *incorrigible*?" I took the longer word slow.

"I can't be improved upon!" Gabe said, proudly, from a few steps ahead.

I wanted to ask more, but I doubted they would enjoy teaching me their language as much as I enjoyed learning languages. Not that I was finding French easy. Emma stopped, and the near collision into Gabe's back brought me out of my thoughts. He looked down the street one way, then the other.

"Don't run until after we get across—Emma."

Emma scoffed at her brother, then gave me a devious look. Oh, we weren't waiting. We stepped up onto the center lane where the trees were planted. As soon as Gabe stepped up, Emma bolted, dragging me along with her. She squealed and ran faster.

"Emma!" Gabe yelled. Seconds later, Gabe's footsteps slapped against the stones behind us. He reached around and snagged us. "Gotcha!" Emma squealed and giggled and kicked her feet as Gabe lifted us. "You're wretched, Emma Dubois. Don't teach your friend bad habits." He set us down once we were in the shade of the first gnarled old tree.

"Oh, I know all the tricks." I looked down at the ground. Green—but short stalks...Interesting.

"Do you now?"

"Mmhmm." I saw him move out of the corner of my eye, but I grabbed Emma and ran deeper into the park.

Emma squealed again as her brother narrowly missed her.

"Hurry, Emma!" We'd lose him after we were through the first few bushes.

"We can't go through there!" Emma yelled.

Too late—we blew right through and out the other side. There were no other shrubs...just a field of the small green stalks. Gabe barreled through the shrub behind us and almost ran us over in the process.

"Emma, we can't run through the shrubs."

"I know. She didn't."

"What is this?" I kicked at the almost dead plants at our feet.

"*La pelouse.* Don't you have it where you come from?"

"We have plants, but nothing this short."

"That's right! Where are you from? What does it look like?"

"Emma," Gabe growled. "Maman told you."

"That's made up, and you know it." Emma stuck her tongue out at her brother. She hooked my arm again and walked parallel to the shrubs until we met a brick path and began following it. "So?"

"What do you mean? What is made up?"

"Madame Josie told Maman you were in an accident in the mountains, and you can't remember anything."

"Oh." I swallowed and looked away. "I can't talk about that."

"Why?"

"Emma, leave it alone."

"Go away, Gabe. You're supposed to leave us alone."

"Sorry, Fille. Emma doesn't know when to quit." With that, he spun on one foot and walked back. "I'm telling Maman!"

A tiny gray animal poked its head out from its hidden hole up in a tree and began scampering down. "What is that?" I pointed to the little thing with chubby cheeks, little paws, and the bushiest tail I'd ever seen.

"That? It's a *écureuil*. You've never seen—"

"What's it doing?" I interrupted her. We watched the little thing climb down, then run past us and into another tree.

"Looking for food, I suppose."

It jumped back down and ran away. I let go of Emma to follow it. The little guy stopped in the open before the next tree and stood up on its back legs. I waited, not daring to move first. It did a few hops and then stopped again, checking on me. When it determined I wasn't a threat, it continued and so did I. We passed three more trees before it jumped in the row of shrubs and emerging garden.

Emma came to a stop next to me and patted her hair to make sure it was still in the braid. "Come, let's find something else to annoy." Emma hooked my arm again.

"A few birds, one of those things on the rope over there might be fun."

Emma giggled. "Those are dogs, and the women attached to them would not be amused."

"What is the difference between mademoiselle and madame?"

"*Un nom sophistiqué pour appeler une femme.*" She'd lost me.

"I think the only word I understood was *nom*. I'm sorry. Usually, I'm better at this. Languages are easy for me, but this one is difficult."

"What languages do you know?"

"Um..."

"I won't tell anyone. Promise."

"I can't tell you...I cannot remember, eh—"

She set her shoulders and dropped her arm out of mine. "Are you a *fée*?"

My heart fluttered. Marie had said that word. "No," I whispered. A little dog growled, accompanied by a lady's gasp and another's laugh. Biting my lip, I refocused on Emma.

"Can you use *la magie*?"

Clueless about that one, I gave her a blank look. Emma pursed her lips. "You're different, there's something about you that feels"—she waved her hand in the air—"different. I feel something in my heart from you that is different than others, and I think it's because you're not human."

"Oh." Was she like Marie? "Are you *fée*?"

"No, we're human. But Maman feels the difference. And Gabriel."

"I'm no different from you or Josephine. Please, forgive me, but perhaps your imagination has..." I waved it off, not caring about the idiom. "I'm a human girl like you. Please believe me."

Emma held her breath. I could see her thoughts shifting by the look in her sparkling amber eyes. "I'm sorry. If you ever want to talk, we won't tell."

I wrung my hands. "I have made things...odd?"

"Let's play, so we don't need to think of it now."

"What do you want to play?"

Emma grinned. "Do you like climbing trees?"

I snorted and ran to the first perfect climbing tree.

Gabriel called us some time later after the women with their dogs left. We heard him, but we were too busy catching *lucioles*—beautiful insects that glowed from their abdomens. At first, I thought they'd burn me, but Emma held my hand and let one walk across my palm. I screamed anyway, as the feel of its little legs tickled. That didn't matter though, catching them was too much fun. Oh, if Nol could see these! I paused. Twynolan. I imagined the wonder in his eyes as Emma tried to explain how it glowed without magic.

Not that I asked if the *lucioles* were magical. From everything I'd seen, the realm held no magic. What *Aore* Junae said was wrong. Or a lie. While the absence of my magic ached and clenched my core sometimes, I didn't regret it. Casting a spell, even to change the wind currents to push the little bugs closer, might have been dangerous.

"You two are going to get me in trouble. Maman said to come home when the lamps are lit." Gabriel swatted at the *lucioles*. "They've been on for ten minutes."

I stilled, and the *lucioles* swirled around me and then off into the twilight. "Your maman and Josephine will be so mad! Emma, we must get back now." I reached for her hand, but she scooted away. "Maman won't be that mad. We can say we lost our sense of time playing with the *lucioles*."

"But that's a lie." Not that I hadn't ever used them on my parents. I couldn't risk losing her, though. "Emma, I want to continue being your friend, and if Madame Dubois is not obeyed, we could risk our new friendship."

"Oh, Maman wouldn't be cruel like that. You're the first friend Emma's made here in a long time."

"All the girls are stuck up, and they want to play dolls and have tea time." She groaned and let go of the bug in her hands. "Let's go."

Our departure wasn't as exciting as our arrival, but as we stepped out of the park, Emma hooked her arm in mine again.

"Great, now I have to deal with two sisters," Gabe muttered.

"Sister?" I looked over my shoulder and up at him.

"He means we will become close friends. Every winter I can come see you, and when Madame Josie releases you after work, we can go play. Perhaps we could even have a playdate during the day."

Like most of Josephine's clients they were winter tourists. "Where do you go other times of the year?"

"We live in Paris, but most winters we come down here to stay in our *apartement*. It's just a few blocks down from your shop."

"Do you visit during any other seasons?"

"We visited once during the summer. Never again. They're dreadfully hot," Gabriel added. "Sorry, but it's true."

"What are your other seasons called?"

"Spring is next. The days will lengthen and flowers will grow and bloom. Autumn is the harvest and when it starts to turn cooler."

"That is like home—" I sucked in my breath. It wasn't home. I was *savilë*. I would honor my country and respect my sentencing. "I shouldn't have said that."

"Not to worry, like I said. We'll keep your secrets."

"We will?" Gabe stuck his head between ours, startling us. Emma squealed yet again and shoved at her big brother. My Emma was a squealer. Perhaps I needed to find ear protection.

Once we reached Josephine's shop, Emma flung her arms out to hug me. Gabe patted me on the head.

"Maybe Maman will let me visit you tomorrow." Emma held her hands together and bounced next to her brother.

"I have work to do." Always.

"Aren't you a little young for the work program?"

"I don't know—that is, I don't know how old I am," I answered Gabe.

"You look five."

"Five?" I placed my hands on my hips and glared at the tall boy. "I'm just short."

"Now you look older than Madame Josie."

I narrowed my eyes at him. "Funny." .

Emma tapped her chin, studying me. "I'd bet...eleven. But you're just short for your age."

Gabe scoffed at his sister's determination. "Five. You're both imma-ture *petite puces*."

"What is that?"

Both children blinked at me.

"*Une puce*?" Gabe shoved his hands in his pockets. "The little black hopping insect that bites you."

"Ew."

Gabe laughed. "Well, go on, Fille—back into your shop. It was nice to meet you."

I almost corrected them, almost told them my name. But I refrained. Even though Emma promised to stay quiet, I needed to be sure.

19

"Fille!" Emma yelled as the shop bell jingled. "Fille!" She ran into my back area. "We're leaving this morning."

"I know." I kept sewing the hem I was working on. "We've known this." Not that I liked it. Emma was my ray of light in this realm. "In fact, shouldn't you be preparing to leave?"

"I did, we're all ready. Can you see us off at the station?"

I stopped sewing. "Emma, I'm working."

Her expression darkened. "Ask Madame Josie if you can go."

"Josephine has been kind enough to let me spend time with you almost every evening for the past two months." And had given me Sundays off. "I can't ask even more from her."

Josephine walked in and leaned her shoulder against the wall at the entrance to my area, her hands in her apron and mischief in her eyes. "What can't you ask of whom?"

"Madame Josie! May Fille see us off at the station?"

"Well..." Josephine drew out the word. "It departs at eight?"

"That's right. Everyone is outside. Papa has rented a carriage to take us to the station."

"I'm concerned for her return. Will it also bring her straight back?"

"*Oui*. Please, can she come?"

"Hurry. You wouldn't want to be the cause for missing the train, Fille."

"*Merci*, Madame Josie." Emma jumped up and down, waving at me. "Come, Fille, hurry."

I didn't need any more persuasion. I set my project in my chair and hurried out. "*Merci*, Josephine!"

Monsieur Dubois stood next to the carriage, waiting to help us climb in. With its cushioned seats, it was so unlike Jean's cart. The family of seven managed to fit in one. Henri, the second youngest, sat in the second-oldest brother's lap. Those two were almost inseparable, as Henri was quite shy and Adrien stood up for him. Gabe sat next to Madame Dubois, and Emma climbed into Claude's lap so I could have my own spot beside Claude. My presence made it even more cramped.

"Maybe I shouldn't..."

"Nonsense. Come and sit." Madame Dubois beckoned me to sit.

Monsieur Dubois climbed in after me and took up the seat beside Gabe, directly across from me. "Comfortable, little one?" The carriage lurched and rocked as we moved.

"*Oui.*"

"You don't have to lie," Claude said, raising his voice enough to be heard over the clomps of the horse's steps. "No one is." He winked at me and tugged on my braid. We'll miss you, *puce deux.*" *Flea two.*

I scoffed. Gabe had started the nickname. Emma was flea one, and I was flea two, the pair of us always jumping together. While I'd realized Gabe, Adrien, and Claude were more my peers than Emma, maturity and education wise, Emma and I connected on an emotional level. She made me smile, laugh, and imagine a future. My night terrors had even decreased these last couple of months, allowing both Josephine and me more sleep. Perhaps that was another reason Josephine let me spend time with Emma.

"I will miss you all."

"I wish you could come with us," Emma said for the hundredth time—or more.

"Madame Josie needs her, Emma."

Claude pressed her legs down to stop them from hitting his shins. "Enough, Emma," he whispered in her ear. No one else heard. My *endaen* hearing, I'd found, was sharper than a human's hearing.

Emma stuck her tongue out at her brother and he pinched her.

"Stop, both of you. I'll send you to your sleeping quarters for the rest of the trip with no supper if you keep fighting."

"There are beds on the train?" The seven turned to me at once, surprised at my ignorance, perhaps.

"Yes, we'll be traveling all night. We must have somewhere to sleep."

I nodded, trying to grasp the concept of the size of these things. The carriage turned a corner, and we were in an entirely different place! The buildings and people and walkways were all similar, but so much more. The palm trees were planted closer together, the pathways were wider, the road smellier.

"Where are we?" Like most of the larger roads in the city, tall buildings loomed over the pedestrians walking past. Tables were tucked up under canopies that stretched along entire buildings. It was such a busy place.

"The is *Avenue de la Gare*, one of the main streets of Nice," Monsieur Dubois said.

Coming up on the left was a building like no other. Six stone steps off the walkway led to three cave-like entrances. Each entrance met at a point above, stretching to the second floor. White pillars upon pillars rose to two towers that pointed to the sky. A round window—or windows?—in the design of a flower was set above the entrance. Gileal would have loved this.

"What is that?"

"*Basilique Notre-Dame de l'Assomption.*"

"Is that the name of it or the function or both?"

They all laughed at me. My second stupid question of the morning.

"It is a church," Madame Dubois said. "Do you not have these where you come from?" She, like Emma—like the whole family—hinted at my origin. None of them seemed to believe my faulty memory ploy. "Surely you remember your places of worship."

"I think so," I hedged.

"Perhaps, if Madame Josie doesn't take you, we can take you next winter."

"Madame Josie is Jewish, right, Maman?" Claude asked.

"*Oui.* Has she taken you with her to worship, Fille?"

"Ah, no."

Madame placed her hand on her husband's shoulder. "My love, we've done a grave disservice to Fille."

He patted his wife's hand. "Let Madame Josie handle it."

Madame Dubois frowned but stayed quiet. She wasn't going to let it go. The carriage made another turn and there, to our right, was a long chain of compartments on wheels laid out in a row. The wheels were set on metal bars on the ground. The carriage stopped at a building with cave entrances similar to the church and a domed top with a clock in front.

"Eight—no, seven...forty-three?"

"Correct, Fille! I'm so proud." Madame patted the top of my head, careful not to disturb my scarf.

The two oldest boys unloaded the family's luggage with the help of two men in impeccable clothes with silver buttons, shiny shoes, and hats with straps under their chins. Emma hooked her arm in mine and pulled me along.

"*Ma puce*, walk in front, so Fille can see the station."

"*Oui*, Maman."

Emma pulled me around and let me gawk. It was built with the same stone material as everywhere else—with horizontal cream lines, arches above the doors, and windows—and all I could think of was Gil and his love of architecture. Once inside, metal beams held up the roof. To my surprise, the roof was not made of a metal material, but opaque rectangular window panels. The train waited in the station for all the people to come out.

Madame and Monsieur settled themselves on a bench and let us explore the platform. Emma and I walked to one end. People stepped in and out of the black compartments, carrying boxes and bags with handles.

"I'm going to miss you terribly until winter. I'll write you every day, Fille."

"It's Hallanevaë," I admitted, my voice just above a whisper.

"What is that?"

"My name is Hallanevaë."

Emma stared, her mouth slightly open. Had I misjudged our friendship? Would she laugh at me for having such an odd name?

"Hall-anna-ne-vaya?"

I winced. "Close. Ha-lla-ne-va-eh."

Emma tried again. "It's prettier than I imagined and so magical! Perfect for you, Ha-ala-neh-vaya."

"But it's hard to say."

Emma winced. "Yes, I'm afraid so."

"And not like other people's names."

She shook her head. "Should we shorten it? How about Hannah?"

I rolled that around in my head. "No. I don't like the nnn sound in the middle."

"Hèléne?"

I'd heard that one before. "Yes, that one."

I jumped as a loud screeching whistle filled the station.

"It's time to go. Come." She dragged me back to her family. In a whirlwind of hugs, cheek kisses, and goodbyes, I found myself waving at Emma's family from the platform after they found their seats. Monsieur Dubois pushed up a window for Emma to hang out of and wave.

"I'll write every day, I promise!"

"Take care," Madame Dubois called out. "We will miss you!"

The train screeched again, and the wheels rolled as it made a deep pulsing thump. Their hands waved and waved until it turned away. I swallowed hard as I tried not to cry. Time to go back. At least I had Josephine. I thanked the Mother that she was nothing like Madame Allard at the orphanage.

"JOSEPHINE!" I CALLED AS I came through the door. "Josephine!" I ran up the stairs into her apartment, where she was making something for lunch.

"How did it go?"

"Trains are huge! And loud. And Madame Dubois wants me to go to a church."

"Well, if you want, I'm sure I can arrange Madame Moraine to take you to hers on Sundays. I've never heard you so talkative, Fille."

"Please…" I wrung my hands a moment, but I had to start trusting some people. "Call me Hèléne."

"Oh, I like that name." Josephine winked and handed me a carrot.

"Emma helped me pick it out. Is it too much?"

"Not at all. Sit and have tea with me, Hèléne. Tell me all about those trains."

20

CHURCH WITH MADAME MORAINE was odd. She didn't go to the one we passed that day to the trains, but I liked the bell. While I found their religion quite confusing—a male god made the world in six days and rested on the seventh. That was why people went to church on the seventh day of the week. He made an apple tree and told his children "Look but don't touch." My question was, how did he have these children if women carried the babies? Where was their mother deity?

But I was learning how to read during church using their bible, and Madame Moraine helped at home. Our routine, as simple as it was, made four months go by fast. Josephine always kept me doing something, even if it was just fetching equipment down the road.

"Hèléne? Is that you?" Josephine called out of her apartment above.

"*Oui*. I brought the groceries." I set down the other items she'd sent me out for and hurried up the stairs. My stomach growled, smelling the herbs and vegetables of our supper even from the bottom of the stairs. "Monsieur Bernard wanted me to say hello to you again. You know, I'm much more comfortable with French now, if you ever want to take a few hours to go visit him."

Josephine scoffed at my teasing. It was becoming a normal thing.

"Oh, come now. You need company."

She turned away from the stove and clasped my arms. "I have you." She kissed my cheeks and took the turnips from me.

"It isn't the same." I pulled out the baguette.

"Nonsense." But I heard the smile in her voice. I'd wear her down soon enough. "Oh, you have another bundle of letters downstairs. Why don't you go get them, and you can read one to me at supper." I'd read her every letter.

"All right!" Emma wrote to me every day, like she'd promised, but sent them out once a week. And eventually I learned enough to write back.With a skip of excitement, I ran downstairs. The letters were in the basket where Josephine always set them after the post arrived.

Something large hit the floor upstairs and a dish clattered. "Josephine?" When she didn't answer, I headed back up, letters forgotten.

She lay on the floor, the pan touching her arm. I shoved it away, burning myself in the process. "Josephine?" I shook her shoulders. I leaned over her face and felt for her breath—nothing. Next, her pulse. I sat back on my heels, without a single idea of what to do next. "I'll get Madame Moraine." I kissed her forehead and hurried out the door.

"Madame! Madame Moraine!" I rapped on the door next to us. She was hard of hearing, and she went to bed quite early. After an eternity, the latch turned and the glow of her candle shone through a crack. "Madame!" I called even before the door was completely open. "Something is wrong with Josephine. She fell and she isn't breathing."

Madame Moraine squinted at me. Her sight wasn't too sharp, either. "Hèléne?" She licked her dry lips. "Heavens, why are you out this late?"

Frustrated, I explained again.

"Oh, no."

"Please, I don't know what to do."

"Go fetch Monsieur Maurice two doors down. Tell him what you told me."

Without another word, I went and rapped on his door. I didn't know this neighbor as well, but there was no time to question if I could trust him. He didn't take as long to respond as Madame Moraine, but by his furrowed brow and deep frown, I knew he hadn't wanted company.

"Monsieur, Madame Moraine sent me. It's Josephine—my—" I didn't know what to call her. "She fell and she's not breathing. Please, can you help?"

A woman's voice from inside made him close the door most of the way. They talked in whispers. She wanted to know who was there, and she was not happy that he'd opened the door.

"Please, Monsieur, I have no one else to turn to."

That did it. He opened the door wide, grabbed his jacket from a hook, and followed me back to Josephine's.

"I don't know what happened. I was downstairs, and I heard a crash. She wasn't breathing, her heart—it's not—um, moving. I'm sorry, I don't know the words." Perhaps on a less stressful occasion, but not now.

"Just bring me to her." I led him up the narrow staircase. The herbs still wafted down the stairs. She'd kissed my checks only a few minutes ago. Monsieur Maurice checked her vitals like I had, sat back on his heels, and then gave me a desolate look, and I knew.

"No. Please, no."

"Do you know any of her family?" he asked.

Tears fell as I shook my head. "What—what do I do?" I swallowed and cleared my throat.

"Ask to stay with Madame Moraine for now. I will inform the mayor and the synagogue."

I nodded but couldn't get up and leave her.

"Fille? Bring your belongings. I'm not sure if they'll let you come back in, as you aren't family."

All of my belongings and bed were hidden from view behind a curtain in my workshop downstairs. I stuffed the bag that Marie gave me...nine months ago? Everything Josephine had provided for me in the last six months went into the bag, now brimming with two sets of decent clothing and a nightgown. I also snuck out a sewing kit.

Monsieur Maurice walked me over to Madame Moraine's.

"I don't have large furniture, so I hope you don't mind the floor," she told me in her shaky voice. "Blankets are in the chest over there." She waved at the chest in the parlor.

"What will happen tomorrow?" I winced as her worn blankets ripped.

"Likely, your orphanage will be told to fetch you. Don't worry, I'm sure they'll find a nice place for you. Have you eaten, dear?" She tossed a throw pillow on the floor.

After a bite to eat, Madame Moraine headed back to bed. The silent home felt as numb as I did. I stared at the carpet in front of me, my thoughts fleeting away before I could grasp them. I saw flashes of Josephine on the floor, or smiling in the shop, working at her bench. I didn't sleep.

The next morning, Madame Moraine made me eat croissants and coffee before the sun was even up. "Hèléne, don't pick at your food, dear. You need to eat."

I pulled off a bigger piece. A knock on the door startled Madame Moraine, and coffee spilled down the side of her cup. "Answer the door, child," she said as she patted her hand dry.

I shuffled through her old apartment, trying not to kick up any more dust than possible.

A portly man of middle age fidgeted on Madame Moraine's stoop. "*Bonjour*, mademoiselle, I am *Maire* Goiran. Are you Madame Josephine's Fille?"

"Hèléne, *oui*. Madame Moraine is this way." I opened the door wider. "Madame?" I rose my voice so she could hear me. "Monsieur—"

"*Maire* Goiran," he snapped.

I waved him back. "Apologies. *Maire* Goiran is here."

Madame set her cup down as we entered, her hands and head shaking as they normally did. Her cloudy eyes rolled up to inspect the mayor. "*Bonjour, Maire* Goiran. Wonderful of you to come so early."

"Yes, best we have this done quickly. Is there anything I can do before I take the child off your hands?"

"Hmm, I think not. Hèléne, would you fetch me my bible in the parlor?"

Nodding, I hurried over, and by the time I'd come back, Madame had found an ink bottle and pen. "Set it on the table and open it to the first page, *ma chère*." With a thin line of ink, in her shaky penmanship, she wrote my name below another's name. "Hèléne, this book has been in my family for generations. It is yours now."

"But your children…Shouldn't it go to them?"

"Édouard wouldn't care, and Éric can have the other one. I think this will mean more to you than them."

"Oh no," I gasped, reminded of the most important thing back in Josephine's place. "My letters."

"Your letters?" *Maire* Goiran asked.

"Yes, in the shop. I forgot the new ones in the post basket."

"Mademoiselle, I cannot allow you back in there."

"But they are addressed to me. Please?"

"It is quite inappropriate to ask me to take something from a deceased person's home, you do know that?"

"I wouldn't ask if I knew I could get them later. Please?" I begged again.

"I will see what I can do. Madame?" *Maire* Goiran gestured for Madame Moraine to lead us out.

She kissed my cheeks as the mayor opened the door. "Good luck, my dear."

"Sit on the steps here and wait for Madame Allard. I'll look to see about the letters."

"They're in a basket in the front, where she collected all her post until she was ready to deal with it."

He pursed his lips and fiddled with his hat for a few heartbeats before stepping into Josephine's home. I sat on those steps and watched Monsieur Maurice walk through and talk to *Maire* Goiran. Some men in black robes, with hairy faces and long locks of hair resting against their shoulders, walked up and spoke with *Maire* Goiran. Still, the mayor didn't acknowledge me.

Black shiny shoes stepped into my line of sight as I stared down at my own boots, hugging my knees and waiting for whatever came next. "Are you Hèléne?"

My head rose to find one of the hairy faced men looking down at me. "*Oui.*"

"I'm Rabbi Judah. Madame Josephine spoke of you often." With the squint of one eye, he dug around in his pocket for something. "I saw these on the table in there, and I believe they are yours?" He handed me the bundle of letters.

"Oh, thank you! I was worried I wouldn't get them." I pressed them to my chest. "I don't think *Maire* Goiran wanted me to have them."

"No one wants Madame Josephine's belongings to be taken by the wrong person. I happen to know she would want you to have these."

The clacking of a familiar set of shoes interrupted our conversation. I looked at Josephine's Rabbi, silently imploring him to take me with him. He gave me a kind smile as Madame Allard stepped into his space.

"*Bonjour*, I'm here to collect *la fille*."

"But of course. Hèléne is right here."

"I'm aware this is the girl," Madame Allard snapped. "Are you the one I must clear it with?"

"One of them. Hèléne, take care of yourself," he responded with more grace than I ever could. "Thank you for giving Madame Josephine some light at the end. She was much happier after you came."

I stood, still trying to silently beg him to keep me there. Anyone but her.

"Do you have a place sorted for her already?"

"Yes. She will be the nanny at Monsieur Laurent's home. The children recently lost their mother."

"Ah. I'm not familiar with him, but I'm certain it will be easy to find if needed. *Bonne journée* to you, Hèléne. *Au revoir*, Madame Allard."

He placed his hands together and bowed his head. Madame Allard's clacking shoes didn't wait for me to say much of a farewell to the rabbi, so I waved and hurried after her.

"You're lucky, Monsieur Laurent recently came seeking help. I haven't any who've aged out. Keep up. Hèléne, huh? Is it made up, or did you remember it? I don't know how many children Monsieur Laurent has," she continued without waiting for me to answer. "You'll have to be firm with them, none of your meekness. That won't do."

21

I'D NEVER DEALT WITH children, and this cemented in my mind, motherhood was never meant for me. Michelle, the four-year-old and third youngest of Monsieur Laurent's nine living children—they'd lost two in infancy— threw her dinner roll at me for the—I'd lost count of how many times. It hit her brother between the eyes. Lawrence screamed. At three, he cried about everything.

"Michelle, we don't throw things."

"Milk!" Her little sister drank the last of the milk with supper. Annette, the youngest, toddled up to me and gave me the bread that her sister threw.

"*Merci.*" I tapped Annette's nose gently.

I'd been missing Twynolan terribly. My energy was down, my attitude was horrible, and I'd developed headaches. The latter might have been the result of dehydration, but eating or drinking didn't sound interesting. Three seasons without him was a feat, but the fact was I'd just gotten used to the empty feeling and night terrors.

Marc Laurent's drinking routine began when he walked through the door. He was usually drunk at the dining table and passed out before the children were in bed. But tonight, Monsieur Laurent sat awake on his chair, staring at the floor in front of him.

"Lily?" Laurent called to his dead wife, his voice slurred. I ignored him as I cleaned the kitchen. He'd pass out soon. "Lily? Get out here, woman."

As I set the last dish in its place, a pot slid and the whole pile of them shifted. I winced at the clatter.

Laurent stomped through the house. "Don't ignore me."

The tiny kitchen had one entrance and no place to hide. I pressed my back against the wall, willing myself to blend in. Laurent stumbled into the kitchen, belly bloated and hunched over, his red eyes locked on me—but not me. His dead wife, whom I suspected had met an unnatural death.

"You know better than to ignore me, Lily." He drooled and slurred his words.

"I'm Hèléne, remember?"

He blinked several times, then dropped his bottle as he rubbed his face. I waited for the chance to slip by him. When he wiped the drool from his chin, I dove around his legs. I nearly made it past him when his foot hit my back. He kicked me again before I could respond. My chin hit the ground and I rolled on my side.

"You don't ignore me when I call you—" He leaned over until his face was above mine, the reek of absinthe on his breath. "Do you understand me, Lily?" His spit fell on my face and I screamed. He lifted his foot, and for a moment I thought he'd stomp on me. I scooted backward, but his other foot connected with my side, once, twice, three times in the same spot. The last kick hit my shoulder.

Grabbing my arm, he dragged me through the house, then turned toward his bedroom. I flailed. This would not happen. I refused to give up. I would not die like Lily. Nol needed me to stay alive.

I grabbed doorframes as we passed, my fingers going numb as he yanked me off of them.

"Papa!" Pierre's crackling, twelve-year-old voice yelled from the boys' room. "Papa, stop!" The brave boy hurried past me and grabbed his father's arm that held me. "Don't hurt her, you'll never forgive yourself."

"Get off me, Pierre." He hit his son across the face and sent him into the wall.

Pierre's head hit after his back, bounced forward, and the boy slid to the floor with his chin on his chest.

"Pierre?" I cried. "Pierre?" Blood dribbled out of his mouth. I filled my lungs and screamed.

Allen, the second oldest boy, came out of the room next, then Brigette. Exhausted from my screaming, I lay there panting while Marc Laurent stared at his son.

"Papa?" Allen, approached his father, but made sure to stay out of arm's reach. "Please release Hèléne and allow me to check on Pierre?"

A gasping, rattling breath came from Pierre. Laurent roared and threw me. I flew into his room. My back hit something hard, knocking the wind out of me. Fearing what he'd do next, I scrambled under the bed.

From under the bed, I watched Laurent kneel near Pierre. Allen and the two oldest daughters, Brigette and Anna, stood over their father.

"Is he dead, Papa?" Claire, his five-year-old daughter said, from their tiny closet room.

Laurent carried Pierre into the boys' room. Brigette and Anna hurried into their father's room. A pair of knees dropped on the floor next to the bed, and then Brigette's face appeared. "Come to our room and hide. He won't come in there."

"How do you know?" I asked.

"Because that's what Papa does."

"Yes," Anna said. "Let's hurry before he comes back."

Anna helped me out, and between the three of us, we made it to the girls' makeshift room and fell on their bed. No sound came from the boys' room. Little arms wrapped around me, then another set. Annette sat on my lap. Anna and Brigette sat next to me, squeezing my hands tight.

"Is Pierre dead?" Claire whispered.

"We don't know. Stay quiet," Brigette said.

"Is that how your mother died?" I whispered. None of them said anything. "We must stop him before he kills someone else."

Brigette scoffed at me, a loud sound that made us all wince. "They won't do anything. We're expendable."

"Children die all the time," Anna added.

"This is going to end. I won't have it."

"And what do you think you'll do about it?"

"I'll figure it out, Brigette."

ANNETTE SLID DOWN MY hip for the seventh or eighth time. I hitched her up and looked to both sides of the busy street.

"Hèléne, we shouldn't have left Pierre by himself." Brigette's voice shook, and not from our hurried pace.

"I'm sorry, Brigette, but it must be this way. I told you I won't let it happen again. Not to me, not to you."

"But you don't even know where this synagogue is!"

"Come!" I grabbed Claire's hand and Brigette hitched Laurence higher. "Hurry, Allen!"

He wrapped both arms around Michelle and ran.

When we left soon after Monsieur Laurent went to work, Pierre was still breathing, wet labored breaths. Brigette knew. I saw it in her eyes as she sat with me on the boy's bed as I checked his bulging red eyes this morning.

"Hèléne, I can't carry her any farther!" Allen cried. We did need a break, not that we had any money for food or drink.

I set Annette down and grabbed her hand. "Come sit against this wall and catch your breaths. The man said we need to cross two more blocks. I'll ask for help again after that."

"I'm thirsty. Will we be there soon?"

"I don't know, Anna."

Last night, listening to their father snore, lying across his bed with a bottle of absinthe in his hand, I decided I needed help. If I was in charge of these children, then their safety was my responsibility. Laurent killed his wife, and soon his son would follow. I wouldn't allow him to kill another one.

When the children's breaths leveled out, I rose and dusted myself off. "We need to keep going."

"Can't we go back?" George whined.

"Hungry!" Michelle shouted. Laurence slapped her and she started crying.

"I want to go back!" George cried, like he was five instead of eight.

"Do as I say." My hands balled into fists and I ground my teeth. Their complaints and questions were getting on my nerves, but it wasn't their fault. I pressed my fingers to my temples. "I'm sorry. My head hurts, and I'm sure yours do, too. Please, do as I say. If this goes as I planned, then everything will be resolved tonight."

"And if it doesn't go as planned?"

"Brigette? *Tu dois être courageuse.*" *You must be brave.* Marie's words echoed in my mind. Words I didn't understand before but I now shared with a thirteen-year-old girl. While not going into exile, Brigette was doing something just as scary. "Now pick up Annette. No, Anna, let Michelle and Laurence walk a while."

Michelle threw a fit at the end of the block, but we kept going. Once she realized we weren't listening, she caught up and stayed quiet—mostly.

Allen sneered. "Why are we going to the synagogue again? We're not Jewish."

"And?" I stopped and reeled on the eleven-year-old boy, who was several inches taller than me. "They are a respectable community that is hardly spoken ill of. Your father's prejudices are hateful and undeserving. If you don't want to go, by all means go home and wait for your father."

"Hèléne? Are you well?" Brigette said.

"No, but once I talk to Rabbi Judah, I think I'll be all right."

"Will he have food there?"

"Yes, George, I've already told you he will."

"Is he kind?" Anna asked.

I took a deep breath and forced myself to calm down. "He was kind to me. Come, save your breath for walking."

The trip took more than time out of us. Exhausted and hungry, we reached the synagogue at sunset. The white stone synagogue, built in the middle of the block, glowed a soft orange in the setting sun. Vast and dark inside, I wondered, at first, if this was a mistake.

"Hello?" A familiar voice echoed from our right...or perhaps in front of us? "We aren't offering soup here."

"Rabbi Judah?" I stepped out and away from the others. "Do you remember me?"

"Hèléne?" Rabbi Judah stopped. "Madame Josephine's worker?"

"That's right. I've come to ask you a very big favor."

THE HORSE WHINNIED AS my feet hit the walkway. I carried no bags nor money to give the driver. That had been arranged by Rabbi Judah. Something shattered inside the Laurent house. I shook the green bottle I'd brought with me, shoved my nervousness down to the pit of my stomach, and set my jaw.

"I'm done," I muttered to myself as I stared at the door. "You can do this, Nevie. It must be done." I set my shoulders and went in.

Pots and pans crashed as I walked around the corner into the tiny kitchen where Laurent was throwing things.

"When you're through with your tantrum, come to the living room and talk."

"How dare you," Laurent roared.

I walked back and waited for him to follow. He growled as he stormed out. I slammed the bottle on the parlor table, and he froze, fixated on the green glass.

The tiny clock in the parlor ticked louder than my breathing as Laurent's shoulders heaved. He scratched his balding head and screwed his brown eyes up as he fought his own nature. I crossed my arms and stared. The clock kept ticking and he kept snatching those glances. The clock moved one hundred ticks before I spoke.

"You have some choices to make."

"I don't take demands from a child."

"Shut up and listen because I'm only going to say this once. I know you killed your wife. Accident or not, you killed her. Pierre is dying, and you only have yourself to blame for that.

"But I will bring your children back if you pledge to abstain. You will bring all your money home for Brigette to manage, as she is the best with math in the household. If you so much as lay a finger on me or any of the children again, your work will be told the truth about Madame Laurent's and Pierre's deaths and of your drinking on the job."

"And if I choose the bottle?"

"You'll never see your children again. You will be a sad, selfish, insignificant man wallowing in his own self-pity for the rest of your very short life. It's your choice."

"Is that a threat?"

"No, it's fact. The absinthe is poisoning your body. I'll be surprised if you see the next decade."

"What now?"

"Your choice. By the way, there's no food because you picked a selfish path and bought alcohol instead of food for your children. Congratulations, you're the picture of fatherhood."

He glanced down at the bottle again. "I don't know if I can stay away from it."

"You know the consequences. Now, I'm going to leave you here to decide. I'll be back in the morning."

"Where are my children?"

"Safe and fed because I took care of them and protected them from you." I knew what he'd choose, and I knew Pierre didn't have a chance, but the children didn't need to know that. As sad as it was, I couldn't stop and think about the sweet twelve-year-old boy who'd risked himself to save me. The rest of the children needed me. I felt like Madame Allard.

Rabbi Judah was waiting for me in front of the synagogue when I returned. He stepped up and offered his hand as I jumped off the carriage. "How did it go?"

"He didn't take it, but the first question he asked was about the bottle."

"And the boy?"

"Rabbi...I didn't need to check on him. You as well as I know his fate. The moment I saw his bulging eyes this morning..." I shook my head. "Pierre can't be saved. I'm just grateful to…God that he has been unconscious all this time."

"Nonetheless, I'll check on the boy in the morning."

"Rabbi—"

"Madame Allard was called. She'll be here early in the morning. It is an unsafe situation that I cannot in good conscience send the children back to. It took all my strength to allow you to go back tonight."

I ground my teeth. The orphanage wouldn't be much better, but I didn't argue. The rabbi had no alternative for them.

"You've changed, Hèléne, since I last saw you."

"Being beaten changes a person. These children needed me."

"You're just a child yourself."

"Honestly, I don't know how old I am." In human years, I added silently. "But I feel older than them."

"I doubt that. You just choose to be a hero and not a victim. It matures people faster."

I didn't respond. I was no hero. Rabbi Judah walked me into his synagogue, where I found the children eating bread with the other rabbis. I wouldn't break the news to them tonight—about their brother and father—not until it was official. I thanked the Mother that Rabbi Judah volunteered to go in the morning. I never wanted to see that man again.

22

"*HÈLÉNE, TU ES LE fléau de mon existence.*" Madame Allard turned to me after she sent the other orphans to show Monsieur Laurent's children their new sleeping quarters.

"I don't know what that means, Madame."

Madame Allard moved around me, her shoes clacking as she walked down the hall toward her office.

"I am sorry about bringing them to your place." I hurried after her so she couldn't close the door in my face. The woman was fast. "You are overrun. I see that you do all that you can for the welfare of us children, and I thank you from my heart for all that you've done for me and every child that has come through those doors."

"*Ne me condescend pas, fille.*" She walked to her table and reached for something underneath her desk. Perhaps I went too far in my gratitude.

"I don't know what that means, either, Madame. After my new experience, I can imagine being responsible for so many and not knowing if they'll survive long, wherever they're taken to. I don't—eh—envy you your job."

She squinted at me. "How old are you?"

I settled my hands behind my back. "I don't know, but Rabbi Judah thinks I'm still young, just not a victim. I didn't like being beaten, so I took control of my situation."

She twisted her lips and thought. "Hmm. I have something for you."

"Oh?"

She pulled out a large stack of papers—my letters to Emma. "Yes. It turns out Monsieur Laurent wasn't sending your letters as he told you."

"What? He said—why would he do that?"

She wiggled the papers over her desk until I took them. "I can't speak for him, but you're welcome to send them now."

I shuffled through the pile. On the bottom I found the first one, the one where I told Emma my new address and what happened to Josephine. "She didn't know...If Emma has been sending my letters to Josephine's place still, would they be there?"

Madame Allard set her pen down and folded her arms. "No. The post would have been returned to the sender."

But if they were sent back, Emma might have stopped. "She sent out a package of letters every week."

"Don't look so pitiful. You have her address, send the letters now—or send a new one explaining the situation. The faster you send a letter, the faster you can get new ones." She dipped her pen and pressed the tip to the paper. "Now we both have work to do."

Squeezing my fists and picturing Marc Laurent's red, drunken face—and perhaps smacking him upside the head with that bottle—I counted until I could think clearly. "Fine. May I have a pen and paper? Please?"

Madame sighed, set the pen down again, and got up. "If it will get you out of here, by all means, yes. But write this on your own time. We all have our work to do."

"Yes, Madame, *merci.*" I snatched the paper, pen, and ink from her. With the letters clutched to my chest and the materials to contact Emma, I ran out and didn't stop until I was at my bed.

"Hèléne? What's wrong?" a girl of ten or eleven asked from across the empty room.

"Nothing now that I have my letters."

"Letters?" The girl, I couldn't remember her name, hurried over. "Are they romantic letters? Tell, please." She shook the dusting rag in her hand in her excitement.

I grabbed the rag before any more dust got on my bed. "They're my own letters, and we'll talk about it at free time." After I'd finished my letter to Emma. "Come, show me what still needs doing."

Dearest Hèlene,

Everyone was so relieved to receive your letter. We feared the worst. When your letters stopped suddenly, I begged Maman to travel there and find you, but Papa said some recent events in Aigues-Mortes has made it too dangerous to travel. He won't say what exactly happened, except it was violent, but he promised me they would consider traveling in the fall.

Then Maman was clever enough to call upon Madame Josie, and then Madame Moraine wrote back to give us the dreadful news that Madame Josie had died, and she did not know where the orphanage placed you next. Rabbi Judah didn't know either, and the letters sent to the orphanage returned unopened! Oh, the despair!

At that juncture, Gabriel offered to take the train down to look for you himself. Maman and Papa refused him. They paid close attention to the post-happenings of the deadly event and Papa said that since there hasn't been much retaliation in the past month, they have decided to go down!

Papa arranged for two managers to oversee his position for five days, which leaves them a full day to search for you. Papa wanted to visit the orphanage in person to demand the information. But there is more! One of our letters was received by the orphanage, and we learned that we were sending our letters to the wrong orphanage! Can you believe it?

And then today, Henri came running through the house, calling "she has written, she has written!" Oh, what joy! Now, since you have been found, Maman and Papa have decided to make a holiday of it. We will all arrive by train on November 25th, and we will spend the day with you! Papa, of course, suggested touring the Château, as he remembers your interest in our histories. He would very much like to expand your knowledge, since history is a hobby of his.

Adrien proposed that we let you choose what to do for the day. What a grand idea! That means you have until November 15th to decide on an activity that you would enjoy doing to ensure Maman and Papa can prepare for the visit. Maman has made it perfectly clear that we will still be buying you new shoes.

Now I must end this letter before the post leaves for the day, as I want this to reach you as soon as possible.

With love from all of us,

Emma Dubois

PS

Maman has requested, if you could, please measure your feet to give to the shoemaker. She says there are no more excuses. She is adamant that your boots must have worn out by now. She promises to find as comfortable shoes as she can.

"That's it?" Anna said after I finished the letter.

"It's two pages long, Anna!" I laughed and shook the pages. "It took me forever to read." The girls began spouting off questions one right after the other until I couldn't decipher one from the other.

"How old is Gabriel?"

"Oh, he must be older if he offered to travel by himself," another of the twenty-nine girls in the orphanage said.

"Emma's handwriting is so lovely. Are you sure she's ten?"

"Rich people all write nice, Jenn."

"That's rude, Alisa."

"Is he handsome, Hèléne?"

"What's today's date?"

"The second—I think," Brigitte answered.

"What happened in *Aigues-Mortes*?" Celeste said, but no one knew.

"Did they buy you these clothes, too?" Brigette pinched the hem of my dress. "Do they come from a wealthy family, or is Monsieur Dubois a self-made man?"

"What do you want to do when they come?"

"Oh, Marnie, how can she know that yet? She just read the letter. But surely, she must have some ideas. Hèléne?" Céline said.

The girls kept chattering like birds, each question falling upon the next one. Madame Allard had stood in the doorway, listening as I read. As the girls' voices grew more excited, Madame Allard raised her chin to me and left, her hard-soled shoes clacking. Then something occurred to me.

"Madame?" I ran after her.

With her hand on the top of the railing, she turned, a sour look on her face as she waited while I hurried next to her.

"Did you know? Of the letters? Was there any word from the other orphanage?"

Her head tilted as her eyes narrowed. "What are you implying? Do you believe I would keep that information from you?"

She knew what I meant. This past week, her attitude had declined to almost the same level as when I first arrived. Did she need more flattery? I'd made sure to help keep the children in line and away from her to let her work. She rarely needed to bark at any of us.

"I hope you wouldn't keep that from me. But it seems odd that no word would have reached you within this past month. Why wouldn't the other orphanage have contacted you, at least to inquire about me?"

"I am a strict director, but I am not cruel." She paused. "No. It is policy not to give out personal information of the children we acquire, for their safety. Some children are abandoned here to protect them from an abusive parent. There are other reasons the where-abouts and other information is not given out. Do you understand?"

I swallowed. "Yes, Madame. Thank you."

She spun around, the clacking of her shoes echoing down the three stories, past the front doors, and down to her office.

"Hèléne!" Anna called. "Come answer our questions. We have so many."

"Yes, and you haven't answered a single one," another girl added. "We want to know more about Gabriel!"

Ever since Celeste heard about my letters the first day, the girls had peppered me with questions until Emma's letter arrived a week later. Being uncomfortable sharing my story, I had given them a brief explanation, but that seemed to fuel their curiosity all the more. Whatever small story they could gleam out of me, quickly spread.

"*Ai*, save me, Mother," I muttered before walking back in to their squealing excitement. Some boys had been interested—in particular, the Laurent children—but the boys had drifted away to make use of their allotted free time before supper.

23

A GUST OF WIND blew through the station, ruffling my skirts. The next moment, the train's whistle blew. Emma's train. A cloud of black smoke billowed out as the huge thing rolled into the station. The high-pitched screech of metal pressing against unmoving metal cut into my ears as if the sound were knives. I covered my ears and closed my eyes. That was worse than when it took off.

"Hèléne!" Emma's voice called, after that murderous noise ended. "Hèléne." There! The smoke was clearing out of the station and I saw her. A hand stuck out of a train window, shaking like a caged bird, as Emma called my name again.

The train station employees gave the all clear, and a moment later, Emma bounded out ahead of everyone. She wrapped her arms around me so tight my shoulders ached. She grabbed my hands and shook my arms. *Oh no!*

"What are you looking for?" Emma asked.

"My—my bag." Behind me, it lay on the ground with my sleepwear peeking out of the top where the buttons had undone themselves.

"*Bonjour, puce deux.*" Gabriel's wild brown hair swung forward to hide his eyes as he reached down to scoop up the duvet pillow cover that was my sleepover bag. He rose to his full height and I held my breath, reminded of Twynolan. Gabe was built thicker and his shoulders were wider, but the movement reminded me of home and my *muranildo.* My lip trembled. "Oh, I didn't realize you missed me that much, little sister."

I shook my head, then laughed at myself. "I missed you all terribly."

"Your French is much better, my dear!" Madame Dubois exclaimed as she came in for a hug, encircling me in her soft, warm embrace.

Henri, Claude, then Adrien all came in for hugs. Monsieur Dubois came last, his hands outstretched to touch my cheeks, before I went to hug him. How had this family become so close to me? I'd done nothing to deserve their love, yet they welcomed me as Emma's winter friend from the south of France.

Emma hooked my arm like she always did. "I am famished! Maman, are we having breakfast soon?"

"After we drop our things off, *puce*. Hèléne, are you ready to spend the night at the apartment?"

"*Oui*. I'm very excited. Thank you for inviting me."

Madame's face fell when she noticed my empty arms. "Where is your bag?"

"No worries, Maman, I have it here." Gabriel squeezed said bag to his stomach. "I wouldn't be a good big brother if I couldn't carry a few bags." Ever since that first evening, Gabriel continued to call me his second sister and himself my best big brother. The others never took mind to it. I was *puce deux* in their eyes.

Monsieur Dubois knelt down on one knee in front of me. "Hèléne, unfortunately, there is business I need to attend to this morning. I hope you won't be disappointed that I can't attend the shopping. With our self-planned holiday, my staff still need help."

"Yes, Antoine and Gabriel will meet us at the *Promenade des Anglais* around twelve thirty, won't you my love?"

"Yes, I promise to be there."

"You can never disappoint me, Monsieur Dubois. You're here, that's more than enough."

"Thank you so much for understanding. I'm excited to show you the Château. Just splendid that you chose to go there."

"Your accent has improved, *puce duex*. Good work." Gabriel winked and patted me on the shoulder.

Arm in arm, Emma and I trailed back as Gabriel and his father fetched two carriages for the family. I looked up at the light gray clouds outside of the station. My breath clouded above me as I exhaled the excrement-filled air that I'd gotten used to assaulting my senses.

"Hey, slow pokes, come here before we leave without you!" Gabriel yelled. Madame Dubois smacked his arm, either for yelling or exaggerating—or both. He smiled at his mother. We hurried to the carriages. Madame gave her husband a gentle peck on the cheek after he helped her up into the carriage.

"Be good, boys." Monsieur glared at his three younger sons.

"Papa, the girls can be just as troublesome as us," Adrien pointed out.

"They'll be busy shopping—you three will be bored and looking for something to do. Listen to your mother."

"Yes, Papa," the boys grumbled.

"Where will we go for breakfast?" Adrien asked as Monsieur Dubois shut the door to dash to his and Gabriel's hired carriage.

"A bakery. We don't want to take too much time. Hèléne has an appointment at nine thirty for her shoe fitting."

"Fun." Claude pinched my cheek. "Good luck getting an opinion."

"Nonsense, Claude, Hèléne has an opinion. But it must be reasonable."

"*Oui*, Madame." I didn't need to have an opinion, not here. "Madame? My boots are still in very good shape."

"Hèléne." She reached over across the carriage and pressed her hand on my knee. "I can understand if they have some significance to you, but they cannot be in that good of shape with these roads."

Like every other pair of my boots I'd ever owned, I would outgrow them before my father's leather protective spell wore off. "They're not bad." I went to lift my skirts above my boots, but she pressed my skirts against my legs. "Hèléne, that isn't necessary." She looked around at the family, who'd somehow seemed to find something else to focus on in this small space all at once.

"I love this." Emma wiggled beside me in Claude's lap, eliciting a hiss from her brother.

"Maman, can we stay at the apartment for your shopping trip? I wouldn't mind watching Henri and Claude—"

Claude snarled. "I don't need babysitting!"

"Neither do I!" Henri chimed in.

"You wouldn't mind watching them, Adrien?" Madame said.

"Maman! I don't need Adrien to watch me."

"Claude, darling, do you remember the last time I trusted you to be home by yourself?"

Claude crossed his arms and stuck out his bottom lip. "That was one time."

"Ha, that month!" Emma laughed, which got her a shove off her brother's lap.

"Maman!" Emma rubbed her backside on the floor. "Now my dress is ruined!" She jumped up as the carriage rocked. I grabbed her arm while she turned. "Look, Maman, is it ruined?"

"No, *puce*. It's just wet. Claude, Adrien will be in charge. I don't want the apartment burned to the ground."

Claude bickered with his mother while Henri insisted he didn't need a babysitter. Adrien sat back and smiled at the chaos, which turned out to be the best idea as I followed Adrien's lead.

"Amazing." Madame Dubois held my boots up for inspection as the shoe store owner helped me into the shoes he'd fit for me. Ones with hard soles. Or rather, hard wooden heels as high as my thumb, while the rest was thick leather and fabric. These would be soiled in a day's worth of walking. Nasty, nasty roads. "Not a worn spot on them."

"I promised you, Madame, I have taken care of them."

"And you haven't grown a centimeter."

"Now, try standing again. The adjustments should give you more comfort," the shoemaker interrupted before I could argue.

"Are the Paris roads this"—I debated on an appropriate word—"crowded with horses and people?"

"Even more so." Madame frowned. "But it is lovely there."

"Motorcars are becoming more popular by the day. Soon they'll replace all the horses and the manure left in their wake." Ah, so the shoemaker understood.

"It is quite a problem." Madame Dubois set down my boot. "Those look lovely on you, *puce deux*. How do they feel."

I wrinkled my nose. "It will take some getting used to."

"Getting used to the heel is the hardest part," Madame Dubois admitted. "I won't make you wear them today. It would be too much walking for the first time with those shoes. Your feet and legs would be in excruciating pain at the end of the day."

I smiled, relieved not to have to wear them.

"DON'T LOOK SO SOUR, your face will freeze like that." Emma laughed at me.

"It will not," I grumbled as I used the mirror to watch the seamstress adjust the sleeves of the dark blue dress they were making me get. They'd planned a surprise dress fitting, giving their seamstress Emma's measurements. They only needed a few small adjustments. "I still feel this is unnecessary."

"You need a new dress." Madame sat up tall and preened. "One for the colder weather."

"Just wait until we wear corsets!" Emma swung her feet back and forth as she watched the seamstress finish.

"That won't happen for a while longer, *puce deux*. Cheer up."

I wouldn't argue with Madame Dubois. She was my lifeline to the human way of thinking, and surviving this place might just come down to clothes, shoes, and corsets.

"Finished!" The seamstress stepped back and held her arms out.

"Marvelous. Now we must get to the park." Madame Dubois stood, but once she met my eyes she stopped and squinted. Uh oh. "Hmm..." Madame twisted her lips as she looked me up and down. "There's something missing."

"What about a headscarf to match, Madame Dubois?" the seamstress asked.

"That's it!"

"A new..." No one had ever questioned my scarves before.

Madame Dubois walked to the partisan. "You can use this for privacy,"

The seamstress handed me a length of delicate, yet firm fabric.

"This is pretty."

Emma pushed me toward the dressing area. "Go!"

The fabric didn't hide my ears. No matter how I wrapped it, their outline still showed. I pulled the scarf off again and sighed. I plaited a wide braid straight down, above my left ear, and then I did one for the other side. With a tight wrapping, the scarf held the braids in place. I let a few tendrils fall loose in the front. It'd work for the day.

I stepped out from behind the partisan to three sets of serious, assessing eyes. "You don't like it? I wanted to do something different for such a pretty scarf."

Madame Dubois clasped her hands together. "It's lovely and very different."

"In a good way," the seamstress added.

"It's perfect for you." Emma tugged on one of my locks in front. "I didn't know it was curly."

Sure enough, it had started curling. "Now that I think about it, most women wear their hair up all the time."

"No. Wear it like that. I love it." Madame Dubois got up from the couch and held her hands out for us. "I don't want to keep the boys waiting too long."

THE MOST SURPRISING THING about the Château was the amount of deterioration that people allowed to take place. *Endai* used magic to preserve things, like my boots, but we—they—also replaced and repaired material often. The Château on the hill was only several hundred years old, and they'd let it fall to ruin in such a short amount of time.

By that evening—and after the most extravagant supper in something called a restaurant—my feet were sore and my legs shook. The heat and state of the castle had made me grumpy by the second hour we'd arrived there.

"Monsieur, I hope you're not upset about my attitude today. I enjoyed learning about the Château. I want to learn more, it's just I'm tired and frustrated." I shouldn't have snapped at the other tourists, but there were so many crammed together and I kept tripping in my dress the entire time.

"But you had a good time, yes?" Monsieur Dubois said.

"The best day I've had in..." I paused to think about how long it had been since I'd enjoyed small, ordinary things. Lessons had taken up most of my time for decades. Enyco and Jemi were there to bully me or Rassel and Asin to accuse me of something—and the stress from such life-changing decisions! It had been too long since I'd enjoyed a day like this. "Years. Thank you for this splendid day, all of you." The carriage jostled, and the horse neighed, eliciting a "oh, oh" from the driver.

"Oh, *puce deux* has become melancholy with this subject. Emma, remind her of all the fun you'll have tonight."

"Oh, *oui*, Maman! We were hoping you would agree to a small *jouer*."

"*J...euer*?"

"*Jouer*," Emma said, correcting me. "Yes, one that you act a part? We can entertain Maman and Papa."

"Emma thinks she'll be an actress in the theater one day."

"No! Stop, Claude. They are just fun."

"Please, say no." Claude held his hands together in front of him as he pleaded.

Emma frowned. "Don't act like you don't like them." .

"They can be fun," Adrien added.

"Henri, what about you?" I asked.

"Me?" The youngest boy went bright red. As a small and shy boy, his siblings often protected him. "Sometimes they're fun. I do the costumes."

"What are costumes?"

They all chuckled. "You'll see." Emma winked. Looked like we were doing a *jouer*...

24

GABRIEL FELL INTO HIS chair again, while I continued to read the script Emma had handed me.

"And you're the mother?" I asked, to confirm.

"That's right." He set his elbow on the back of the chair. Sweat beaded on his forehead and he pinched the dress Henri had picked out for him.

I shook the papers. "Why would you send your child off all alone into the woods, knowing there was a...wolf problem. What's a wolf?" Who does that?

"It's just a story." He leaned the other way and checked on a sibling.

"Stories have lessons behind them, don't they? Is the lesson how *not* to be a responsible parent?"

Gabriel's eyes narrowed, but his mouth twitched as he fought a smile. "Just read the script."

"I am," I grumbled. "What is a huntsman?"

"Someone who cuts down trees for a living."

I gasped. "People make a living cutting down trees? How many do they cut down?"

Gabe snorted. "Where else do you think we get the wood for buildings and furniture?"

"But..." I paused to gather my thoughts. "You use stone for the buildings. Do you honestly need so much wood?"

"Do you have any idea how many people are in the world?"

"I..." I considered Nice and all the inhabitants and my minuscule knowledge of this world. "I have no idea."

"There's something close to one point two million."

Yeah, like I understood that. "I'll take your word that that's a big number until I learn more French. How many—no, wait, I'll figure that out later, too."

"I don't get it." Was he finally coming to his senses?

"The story?"

"No. You. Sometimes you act Emma's age, but then other times you're more mature."

Obviously, *endai* matured at a much different rate—the decades versus years notwithstanding. "Let's refocus on this."

"What's it like where you're from?"

I shifted in my seat and pursed my lips. "Constant darkness and it rains blood. Everyone walks on the ceiling and eats their own toes."

Gabe smirked as he glanced at my feet. "Read the script."

"Bravo!" Madame yelled. Monsieur echoed her as they clapped and clapped, with proud smiles on their faces, like this was the best performance they'd ever seen.

Henri's creations were quite well done with the limited equipment to choose from. Emma didn't play the best Red Riding Hood girl, as she couldn't stop smiling, even as she pretended to be scared of the wolf. Claude—poor boy—suffered through the whole event without complaint.

Gabriel and Adrien grabbed the furniture and began moving it back. Henri tugged on my grandmother costume until I pulled off the apron and sleeping cap. They deconstructed their theater without arguing. Feeling useless and lazy, I walked over and took one of the blankets—Claude's wolf costume—and folded it.

"You did a great job with the costumes, Henri. You have a talent here."

"Thanks." He smiled a toothy grin, some teeth much bigger than others. "Emma makes me do it all the time."

"Do you ever want to play in them?"

His eyes widened and his cheeks flushed. "No. I'd forget my lines. Besides, one time, Claude tried picking the costumes..." He shuddered. "Never again."

I wrapped my arms around my middle and laughed, picturing Claude choosing costumes. "I can only imagine."

Henri laughed too as he shook out his blanket.

"What are you two laughing about over there?" Madame Dubois said. "And why aren't we in on it?"

"Nothing, Maman. Costumes and such."

"Hmmm. Well, it's time to get ready for bed."

"Ugh. Maman! I'm not tired."

"I don't want to hear it, Henri!"

Henri set his blanket with the others and moped out of the parlor. "*Oui*, Maman."

"Come, Hèléne." Emma came over and pulled me into the bedroom. "I'm sorry we have to share the room with the boys, but this is only for winter vacations."

"There's no need for an apology. You could fit two of Monsieur Laurent's homes in this." Josephine's apartment above her shop wasn't big either, but it was better quality than the Laurent's. Even the room behind my workplace was better than the girls' closet.

"Oh..." Emma pulled out her nightgown from a drawer and shook it. Without another word, she walked behind the two-panel partisan in a corner.

"Emma?" I bit my bottom lip and waited. "Emma, I didn't mean to upset you."

"You didn't."

Right, and the whole "quiet Emma" was normal? "You aren't acting like yourself. I only wanted to explain that there's no need to apologize."

"I know." Emma popped out, dressed for bed. She tugged on her nightgown in a few places. At ten years old, she was beginning to show signs of maturity. While I was further along than Emma, it had taken me a decade to get to the point she'd achieved in less than a year. Emma twisted her hands with a downcast look. "I need to get my robe. Do you have one?"

I shook my head.

"I'll see if Maman has something you can use." She dashed out without another word.

When she left, I grabbed my nightgown and scarf from earlier and ducked behind the partisan. I shook out the simple dress I'd worn under my grandmother costume and tossed it to hang over the top. Emma came in as I pulled the scarf off my head.

"Are you dressed? Maman found a robe—it's more of a shawl, but it'll work for you tonight." She stepped behind the partisan and looked up from the clothing she held.

My hands froze in the last few parts of my braid, ears on display.

Emma gasped, her hand over her chest. "Yes!" She jumped up and down, squealing.

"No." I covered my ears and pressed myself against the wall.

"Oh, I knew it. Come." She grabbed my wrist and pulled on my arm. "I'm so happy you've decided—"

"Emma!" I yanked my arm back. "This isn't—"

"This is fantastic. Maman will be so happy. Everyone will be."

"What do you mean?"

Emma grabbed my arm again and pulled. "Maman! Maman! It's true."

"No!" I hissed.

"Hèléne has revealed herself."

Wait. Revealed?

Emma pulled me in front of her mother and father, both of whom still sat in their chairs. Madame's eyes—full of confusion and curiosity—shifted from her daughter to me.

"Emma, love..." Madame raised her hand to cover her daughter's mouth. "Perhaps you were too hasty."

"What?" She stopped and let go of me.

The entire family's eyes were on me. Claude, Adrien, Henri, and Gabriel had all come over, dressed and ready for bed. Gabe's eyebrows drew together as he listened to his mother. Adrien assessed the situation on the side, with Henri hiding behind him. Claude bounded forward to stand beside his mother, hands on his hips as if he knew what all the fuss was about.

Madame Dubois held her hand out to me. "*Puce deux*—"

Monsieur Dubois stood up. "Claude. Go stand with your brothers. Emma, you shouldn't have brought her out."

"But Papa, she's—"

"Hèléne, come here." Madam called me closer. "Boys, bed. Now."

The boys fled the room at their parents' sharp words. Madame held her hands out to us while their father walked into the kitchen.

"Hèléne, don't be frightened."

Emma stepped away and faced me, her excited expression deflated. "Hèléne?"

"No harm will come, *puce deux*." Madame Dubois assured me with a soft look in her eyes. "We've known there's something different about you since we first met you."

"Different?" This was more than that. "Madame—"

"We felt it. You aren't human."

"Yes, we feel it. Here." Emma pressed her hand to her chest. "In our hearts." As she'd said the first evening we spent together.

"I don't"—Monsieur Dubois chuckled walking back in from the kitchen—"but I believe them."

I frowned from one to the other. "What do you mean?"

"The children and Ellie feel your…otherness." He used his pipe to point at us. "Not me, not Josie. I think it's a unique feeling."

Madame pressed her hand to her heart and sighed. "I believe God sent us to Josie's that day to find you."

"To think, we were going to go to my grandfather's house last winter," Monsieur added.

Emma's hands settled on my right shoulder as she leaned against my other side. "Yes, but then I asked to go south. And I love going to grandfather's! But something pulled at me—"

"Pulled at us all. And Antoine listened." Madame's fingers curled around mine. "We don't know exactly, but there's something in you that called us to you." Her chin lifted as she looked at my ears. "You're safe with us." Madame's eyes darted to her daughter. "But Emma should not have pulled you out here. Obviously, you weren't ready to tell us."

Emma dropped her arms from around me. "I thought with your scarf off and your braids out..." Her face fell further and her voice faltered. "I assumed that you were going to tell us. Please, forgive me?"

And here I'd been trying to figure out a way to apologize to her after I'd hurt her feelings. I looked from Emma, to her mother, then her father. "I don't know—"

"There is no need for an explanation, *puce deux*."

"Can we come out yet?" Claude yelled from the room.

"Go to bed!" Madame snapped at them.

"But Emma was the one who messed it all up!" he yelled. "Why does she get to stay out there?"

"I should go, too." Emma began to turn away.

I pounced and wrapped my arms around her. "Don't be sad, Emma. You were excited. I'm not cross, just...nervous. People aren't supposed to know."

Emma paused only for a moment before she squeezed me back.

"We'll keep your secret, *puce deux*," Madame said. "You hid well. This?" She waved at my ears. "This proves that our hearts were right."

"There's more to it than that," Monsieur Dubois said. "I've done some research since we met you. I can show you the books I've found when we—"

"Antoine, not yet."

Monsieur's eyebrows rose high into his thinning hairline. "Later, of course. The point is, there's no reason to hide from us. Whatever you want to say, whenever, and how much are up to you."

I licked my lips "Well, then...um...if you know that, I should tell you a few things. To help you understand...me."

Madame grabbed my hands, preventing me from wringing them further. "You don't have to say anything."

"But, it would..." I looked up at the ceiling as I searched for the right words. Even in *Aemirin* I was at a loss. "It doesn't seem right to keep a few things from you, if you know..."

"Very well, then." Madame adjusted her position in her chair as Emma found a place beside her mother on the floor. "We're ready to listen."

I chuckled, but it wasn't funny. No, this would send me right out their door. "So, um—the reason I'm here..." My head dropped, and I couldn't look at anything but my toes and the nightgown above them. "I made a mistake and it cost my friends their lives. As a result of my reckless actions, they banished me. I can't ever return." The silence was unbearable, so I scrambled for something else to say. "I never meant to hurt anyone."

"Hèléne—"

"It didn't—"

"Hèléne? Did you have hatred and anger in your heart when it happened?"

"No, Madame." I straightened my shoulders, adjusting to the odd question. "It was supposed to make them laugh—and it did! At first."

"God says He judges us, it isn't our place to do so."

I held up a finger. "It does say that in the Bible. But I'll understand if you feel uncomfortable with me around your children."

"I know you're a good person, Hèléne." Madame reassured me. "Your actions prove it every day."

"Oh." I swallowed. "Two more things"—I held up two fingers—"I feel you should know. You keep referring to me and my age and my culture...Well. The truth is, where I'm from, I'm considered a child still. We mature differently. Slower. So I hope you'll take that into consideration when I tell you my true age." Again, I swallowed and licked my lips. *Here it goes...* "Please, understand my people grow much older and mature much slower. We live for roughly twelve centuries." I let that sink in. At first, they nodded.

"Wait—what? Twelve—" Monsieur stuttered as he realized what that meant.

"Centuries. Yes. Twelve hundred years."

Monsieur's head dipped forward as he spoke. "Years."

"Yes."

"And how old are you?"

"I'm almost thirteen decades."

Monsieur bit the tip of his pipe. "You're saying you're one hundred and thirty years old?"

I scrunched my nose up, knowing how absurd that sounded to someone who was only thirty, forty, or however old they were. "One hundred and twenty-eight as of this past spring."

He set his pipe down. "That's somewhat older than you look."

"To a human," Emma said. "Papa, Hèléne isn't human."

"I know, *puce*. It's a shock."

"Is this too much?" I winced.

"A bit." Madame shook her shoulders. "Two big revelations is enough for one night, wouldn't you agree, Antoine?"

Monsieur rubbed his eyes. "I agree."

"Hèléne, would you be hurt if you let us sleep on this before we discuss any more?"

I blinked fast and took a deep breath in. "Do you—should I go back to the—"

"Oh! No, dear. To bed. We'll talk more later. You're safe, remember?"

Monsieur stood and held his hand out to his wife. He took a deep breath. "Everything will be fine, little one."

"Good night, Papa, Maman." Emma snatched my hand and dragged me through the apartment before the adults said anything else.

"There is no way you are one hundred and twenty-eight," Gabriel announced upon us entering the bedroom.

I wasn't surprised that the boys had eavesdropped. "Do you not believe any of it?"

"Of course I do. But little sisters aren't allowed to be older than their big brothers."

"Right. It's a good thing we're not related then."

"If we were...what you are, how old would we be?" Adrien asked from his bed.

I tapped my chin. "Emma would be about one hundred ten, one twenty. Adrien? You would be somewhere in your fifteenth decade and Claude...one hundred."

"Hey. I'm not younger than Emma!" Claude squinted and I winked to show him I was joking.

"So, I'd be a hundred and sixty then, because I'm sixteen?"

"No, Gabe, you'd be fifty."

"Fifty?" Then he closed his mouth and shook his finger. "Funny."

Emma giggled. "Because you said she was five."

Gabe snagged her and rubbed his knuckles on her head. "I know, Emmaline."

"Do you have magic?" Henri asked.

"No. It's complicated. My people exiled me, and I took my magic away so I could never hurt anyone again."

Henri frowned. "So you had magic? But now you don't."

I swallowed and looked away. "*Oui.*"

Claude scoffed. "No doubt, Henri. There's no magic here. How can she have powers when there's no magic? Don't ask stupid questions."

"It's not stupid! You're stupid." Henri stuck his tongue out. Claude scrunched his nose, distraction created.

Emma pushed her way out from Gabe's arms. "Oh! I bet they don't have squirrels or dogs there!"

I laughed and swiped at my wet eyes. "We have birds, though."

"Cats?" Henri asked.

"None of those either. We do have dragons."

They all perked up, breathless as they waited for more.

"Well, then tell us!" Gabe shooed me to keep going.

"Are there princesses, too? Do dragons steal them like in fairy tales?"

"Why would—no, Emma. There are many kinds of dragons. Some as big as a building and some so tiny they'd fit in my hand."

They stayed enraptured as I told them all about dragons. If Henri pressed the magic subject, the others distracted him with another dragon question, until he passed out and we pondered why Earth didn't have dragons.

That was easy. They'd eat the little dogs on ropes.

25

HALF ASLEEP, WE STUFFED ourselves into one carriage the next morning. The station was getting closer. I couldn't see it, as my head was mostly on Gabe's shoulder and his head was on mine, but I could sense it. Dread weighed in the pit of my stomach, but I had to be strong and wait.

I tugged my bag tighter—Madame had bought me a real one to hold my dresses in. Even more exciting, she'd bought me new stamps. I would take the letters to the post office myself, no matter where I went. The carriage jostled a little too hard, and the horse neighed louder than normal. We came to a halt and everyone's heads popped up.

Henri rubbed his eyes. "Are we there?"

"Stay put, children. Come out with us, *puce deux*." Monsieur climbed out and helped Madame, then me, out of the carriage. I needed the help now, thanks to my longer skirts. Ugh. I blinked the sleep out of my eyes and let them adjust to a cold, blue November sky.

"This is the orphanage. I thought I was seeing you off." I wanted to go to the train!

Madame reached for my hand and patted it. "Come with us for a moment. There's something we must discuss with Madame Allard."

"Do I still get to see you off at the train station?"

"Yes, you'll come to the station with us."

Monsieur pulled open the tall wooden front doors. Madame Dubois stood in front of me, blocking my view of the entrance hall. I blinked as my eyes readjusted again.

"Surprise!" the children—all the boys and girls—shouted at me, whooping and clapping. I couldn't move, I'd never heard such noise in my life. Monsieur Dubois grabbed both my shoulders and pushed me ahead of him through the doors.

Monsieur and Madame smiled at the boisterous children. So, this was a good thing? Then I caught sight of someone off to the side of the group who wasn't cheering; well, Madame Allard clapped small and fast hand movements, but that was all.

"What's going on?" I said to Monsieur and Madame Dubois.

Madame Dubois reached for my hand again, and Monsieur squeezed my shoulders. Behind the children, Madame Allard watched the scene with a neutral expression. She'd never let us do this before. What in the Starless Abyss was going on? After a few moments, Madame Allard leaned down and picked up a bag at her feet. *My* bag. As she came forward, the children settled down enough for her to speak.

"Hèléne, you seem confused about the circumstances before you—as expected, since the Dubois's wanted to keep it a surprise. So, it is now my honor to congratulate you on your new placement." She stepped forward and handed me the bag Marie had given me months ago, full of what, by the heft of it, was everything I owned.

They'd not given me a hoorah when Nicole and I left the first time. "I don't understand." I looked at Madame Dubois for answers. "Madame? What's going on?"

"Fille Unetelle?" Madame Allard spoke again into a now silent crowd. "From today forth, you are now Hèléne Dubois."

The room erupted in noise again. Anna ran up and wrapped her arms around my middle and squeezed. "I'm going to miss you."

Brigette pulled me in for my second hug as I stood clueless. "Thank you for bringing us here, Hèléne."

A gust of cold air tickled my neck. Monsieur Dubois held the door open and Madame turned to walk through.

"Madame?" I reached for her once Brigette let go. "I still don't understand."

"You're coming home with us." She took my hand and pulled me through. Monsieur continued to hold the door open as all the children followed.

Madame stayed home and took care of the children. From what Emma told me, they had someone help clean their house. "I'm going to work for you?"

"We've adopted you," Monsieur explained like I knew what adoption meant. No one spoke of adoption. Was it another type of placement?

Celine and Claire came over together.

"I don't want you to go," Claire cried.

Celine grabbed my free arm and shook it. "Hèléne! You're going to be so happy with your new family."

"We must go, or we'll miss the train!" Madame said.

I turned away and hurried to follow. Trains waited for no one, as Monsieur always said. I stopped, and my hand jerked in Madame Dubois's. The Dubois children stood in front of the carriage, holding up a long rectangular piece of fabric. Claude and Emma held one side, Adrien and Henri on another, and Gabriel grasped the middle. Emma dropped her corner when she bounced in place, and Adrien fumbled for it. I looked from the siblings down to the cloth they held and the words written across it.

"BIENVENUE DANS LA FAMILLE HÉLÈNE DUBOIS!"
WELCOME TO THE FAMILY HÈLÉNE DUBOIS

"Madame?"

Madame Dubois turned away from her excited children and wiped a tear from her eye. "Say you'll have us? I want you so much to be a part of our family."

"You are serious?"

Madame and Monsieur bent over on either side of me. Her cheek pressed up to mine. "Please tell us you're not disappointed?"

"That's what I went to do yesterday morning. Gabriel and I came here, and I signed the papers."

Emma's squeal warned us moments before she crashed into me. "You're my sister now, for real." She squeezed my neck and hopped around.

Gabriel walked up behind Emma with a piece of paper in his hand. "Move over, Emma, I want to hug my other little sister, too."

Emma didn't let go. The other boys dropped the cloth and ran over. Gabriel swooped in and grabbed both of us but set us down as Emma squealed again.

"See? I told you I'm your best big brother." He handed me the paper. "It's official. Look."

I lowered the paper with all the confusing words. "Madame Dubois, don't joke."

"I'm not. Please call us Maman and Papa. We want you to be our daughter."

Emma stopped hopping and tugged at my hand. "I can't wait to show you our room. Maman bought you a white duvet that matches mine. I hope you love it. Oh, Hèléne, this will be so—" She squealed again. "Come!" She pulled, but I slipped my hand out of hers and turned to Madame Dubois, who held her hand out to me.

"Exile or not, *puce deux*, you have a family with us."

I jumped and hugged her with all my strength, not wanting to let go, ever. But then we'd miss the train and I wouldn't see their house in Paris or meet Emma's friends.

I was Hèléne Dubois, Eleanor and Antoine's daughter. Despite them knowing what I was and what I'd done. Last night, I'd thought Madame—Maman would throw me out when she learned everything. But instead, they were bringing me into their family.

In spite of what the *Amura Ore* wanted, I had people who accepted me, a family to live with. And I wouldn't be alone.

AUTHOR'S NOTE

Enjoyed this book?

I'd be so grateful if you could leave a quick review or rating wherever you buy your books. Reviews help other readers discover The Exile's Paradox — and they mean the world to me. The QR code will take you a link to find your favorite place to leave reviews and ratings. Thank you so much for reading.

Want more? A Twisted Fate is the first in The Exile's Paradox series and starts 119 years after this book. That's right, Nevie is all grown up and goes by Hally. She's sassy, strong and knows what she wants in life. She's made a life among humans and everything is about to come crashing down. Subscribe to my mailing list and get the first 5 chapters free. https://kristineendsley.com/subscribe/Make sure to tell me what you think once you're done!

ACKNOWLEDGEMENTS

If it weren't for the people here, I would never have published my first book, let alone this one. Thank you.

My critique group at Café Noir in Silverdale. My partner at CritiqueMatch, Rachel. Katie Cross, you are super woman! I wouldn't have done this without your encouragement and advice from you and G.S. Jennson.

My betas! I begged and bugged you to read this and give me your honest feedback. And holy shit, you did! You all rock: Tami, Nikki, Barb, Sarah Stephanie and Cassie.

Adam, I love you. Thank you for coming with me to Miscons, listening to me rant or ignore me when I talk to myself, not complaining when you get up for work and I've just gone to bed, and for being my partner for the past twenty-two years.

My boys, you are my world. You amaze me; you inspire me. How did I get so lucky to be your mom? Thank you for being there, for the hugs and Eskimo kisses.

My editor, Jennifer Griffin. Thank you for making it look professional, you know it'd be a mess without you.

My cover illustrator/designer, Cristiana Léone, thank you for making this book look so magical!

ABOUT THE AUTHOR

Kristine Endsley lives in Western Washington with her husband and two boys, two lazy old dogs, and two wild black kitties. She works as a substitute para-educator to fund her writing habits.